Enrollment Form

☐ **Yes!** I WANT TO BE A *Privileged Woman.*
Enclosed is one *PAGES & PRIVILEGES™* Proof of
Purchase from any Harlequin or Silhouette book currently for
sale in stores (Proofs of Purchase are found on the back pages
of books) and the store cash register receipt. Please enroll me
in *PAGES & PRIVILEGES™.* Send my Welcome Kit and FREE
Gifts — and activate my FREE benefits — immediately.

More great gifts and benefits to come.

NAME (please print)

ADDRESS   APT. NO

CITY   STATE   ZIP/POSTAL CODE

PROOF OF PURCHASE
Pages & Privileges
~~ONLY~~

NO CLUB!
NO COMMITMENT!
*Just one purchase brings
you great Free Gifts and
Benefits!*

Please allow 6-8 weeks for delivery. Quantities are limited. We reserve the right to
substitute items. Enroll before October 31, 1995 and receive one full year of benefits.

Name of store where this book was purchased_____

Date of purchase_____

Type of store:

☐ Bookstore   ☐ Supermarket   ☐ Drugstore

☐ Dept. or discount store (e.g. K-Mart or Walmart)

☐ Other (specify)_____

Which Harlequin or Silhouette series do you usually read?

_____

Complete and mail with one Proof of Purchase and store receipt to:

U.S.: *PAGES & PRIVILEGES™*, P.O. Box 1960, Danbury, CT 06813-1960

Canada: *PAGES & PRIVILEGES™*, 49-6A The Donway West, P.O. 813,
North York, ON M3C 2E8

HP-PP5B

The Story So Far...

After her father's death, Gemma Smith found a flawless black opal—which she sensed could be worth a fortune—and an old photograph that made her realize she could be almost two years older than her father had led her to believe.

Gemma left the outback to find out more about her real identity, and met Nathan Whitmore, a successful playwright and heir to Whitmore Opals, his family's gem-dealing company. Highly attracted to Gemma and struck by her vulnerability, Nathan offered her a reward for the black opal, which he had an inkling had been stolen from Byron Whitmore, his adoptive father, twenty years before. Nathan also offered Gemma a job and a home. Gemma found herself falling for her new protector, though various members of the Whitmore household warned her that Nathan was just a heartless seducer.

But then, to Gemma's delight, Nathan proposed, though he insisted that their engagement be kept a secret. Gemma began to have doubts. How well did she know her husband-to-be, and would their marriage lead to the same kind of love and happiness that Nathan's adoptive sister, Jade, had found with Kyle Gainsford, who had hidden his real-life wealth while he worked as Whitmore's marketing manager? And still Gemma was no nearer to unraveling the secrets of her real origins—or that priceless black opal....

Dear Reader,

Welcome to the third book in a new and totally
compelling family saga, set in the glamorous,
cutthroat world of opal-dealing in Australia.

Laden with dark secrets, forbidden desires,
scandalous discoveries and happy endings,
HEARTS OF FIRE unfolds over a series of
six books, from now until December. Beautiful,
innocent Gemma Smith goes in search of
a new life, and fate introduces her to
Nathan Whitmore, the ruthless, talented
and utterly controlled screenwriter and heir
to the Whitmore opal fortune.

Throughout the series, Gemma will discover
the truth about Nathan, seduction, her real
mother and the priceless black opal. But, at
the same time, in each novel you'll find an
independent, fully developed romance that can
be read on its own, revealing the passion,
deception and hope that has existed between
two fabulously rich clans over twenty
tempestuous years.

HEARTS OF FIRE has been especially written
by one of romance fiction's rising stars for you
to enjoy—we're sure you will!

THE EDITOR

MIRANDA LEE

Passion & the Past

3 HEARTS OF FIRE

Harlequin Books

TORONTO • NEW YORK • LONDON
AMSTERDAM • PARIS • SYDNEY • HAMBURG
STOCKHOLM • ATHENS • TOKYO • MILAN
MADRID • WARSAW • BUDAPEST • AUCKLAND

ISBN 0-373-11766-3

PASSION & THE PAST

First North American Publication 1995.

PRINCIPAL CHARACTERS IN THIS BOOK

Gemma Smith-Whitmore: after her father's death, Gemma discovers a magnificent black opal worth a small fortune, and an old photograph that casts doubt on her real identity. In search of the truth and a new life, she goes to Sydney, where she is seduced by and then married to Nathan Whitmore.

Nathan Whitmore: adopted son of Byron Whitmore, Nathan is a talented playwright, but, after a loveless childhood, he is also ruthless and utterly controlled. Will he ever be the loving, caring husband of whom Gemma has dreamed?

Melanie Lloyd: housekeeper at Belleview, Melanie is emotionally dead after the tragic deaths of her husband and only child. She believes that no man will take an interest in her now...until Royce Grantham strides into her life!

Royce Grantham: a recently retired British Formula One racing champion, Royce travels the world collecting rare and beautiful things. When he sets eyes on Melanie Lloyd, he has to have her, too, not realizing that he will have to battle to win her love and trust....

Ava Whitmore: Byron's much younger sister, Ava struggles with her weight, spinsterhood and fear of failure.

Byron Whitmore: recently widowed, he is the patriarch of the Whitmore household, and a stranger to love.

Jade Whitmore: the only daughter of Byron and Irene (née Campbell) Whitmore, Jade was a wild child until she joined the family business and became assistant to Kyle Armstrong, the company's marketing head. Now she and Kyle are engaged, and she is expecting his baby.

Kyle Armstrong (Gainsford): the head of marketing at Whitmore Opals, Kyle has revealed himself to be the Tasmanian heir to Australia's largest fortune.

Celeste Campbell: the head of the Campbell Jewels empire, Celeste is not to be toyed with. Beautiful and predatory, her heart hides an old love that has twisted her vision....

Damian Campbell: younger brother of Celeste, he is the sales and marketing manager for Campbell Jewels. Interested only in self-gratification and sexual pleasure, Damian doesn't care whom he hurts in their pursuit.

A NOTE TO THE READER:

This novel is one of a series of six novels set in the glamorous, cutthroat world of Australian opal-dealing. It is the author's suggestion, however, that they be read in the order written.

FAMILY TREE

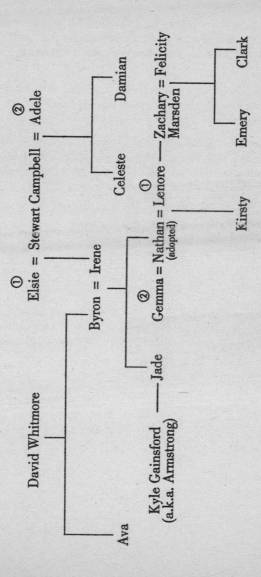

CHAPTER ONE

ROYCE took one look at the huge black opal on display in the shop window, and wanted it.

He'd always been like that. Swift and sure about deciding what he wanted, and obsessive about gratifying those wants. As a ten-year-old boy he'd wanted to be go-cart champion of the English Midlands. By fourteen, he was. Nineteen saw him coveting the world championship in formula-one motor racing.

This time, however, it had taken him thirteen years to achieve his ambition. Thirteen long, hard, dangerous years. He'd subsequently gone on to win the championship in back-to-back years, then stunned the motor-racing world by announcing his retirement. But what had been the point of going on? The challenge had been met, the wanting satisfied. Time to move on and find a new goal.

That had been eighteen months ago, during which time he'd been travelling the world, seeing all those places he'd never really seen from behind the wheel of a racing car. He'd also developed a penchant for collecting antiques and art and artefacts. Already, he'd sent home crateloads of treasures to help fill the sixty rooms of the eighteenth-century Yorkshire mansion he'd purchased two years ago, and to which he would soon return.

Now that he was no longer risking his neck every week by hurtling round a track at two hundred miles an hour, friends thought he might contemplate marriage and a family. But marriage had never been, and never would be, on Royce's 'most wanted' list.

His gaze returned to the opal in the window, while his mind drifted off on a tangent. He started wondering what Australian women would be like. Not that he'd had time to meet any yet.

He'd only landed in Sydney the previous afternoon, the hire car bringing him straight from Mascot Airport to the Regency Hotel where he'd flaked out till late this morning. He'd just been for an after-brunch stroll, and had been wandering past the shops in the foyer of the hotel on his way back to his suite when the opal in the window had caught his eye.

His eyes refocused on the sign sitting on top of the security glass box that housed the large chunk of gemstone. It said:

The Heart of Fire. A rare and precious pinfire black opal of 1260 carats, to be auctioned as an uncut collector's piece at the Whitmore Opals Annual Ball to be held in the Regency Hotel ballroom on Friday night, July 21st. Tickets for the ball may be purchased within or at the Whitmore Opals store on the Rocks. The belle of the ball will be presented with a magnificent solid opal pendant valued at ten thousand dollars.

An auction, Royce mused. On the twenty-first of July. That was over a month away, well after he'd have moved on to Melbourne. Still, from his experience, an item being auctioned did not preclude an interested party making a bid beforehand. He would simply make an offer that the head of Whitmore Opals could not refuse.

Royce was wondering who the head of Whitmore Opals was and how much money it would take to get what he wanted when his attention was captured by a woman standing at one of the counters inside the shop— a black-haired, black-eyed woman with skin like porcelain and a face that belonged to an Italian master's painting. She was talking to one of the salesgirls, showing her something in a plastic bag.

Royce was entranced by her lovely but rather serious face. Her eyes, especially, reflected an inner sadness. A remoteness. He was thinking he'd never seen such an odd combination of beauty and bleakness, when suddenly she smiled, a smile so vibrant and stunningly sensual that he was powerless to stop the automatic response of his male body. Royce's wanting the opal immediately took second place behind a more immediate and primitive want.

With a surge of adrenaline setting his blood racing, he watched her covertly through the window, his mind searching for some way to meet her, his narrowed eyes roving over her now with a more intense awareness of her physical beauty. Never had he seen a face so perfect, a neck so elegant, a mouth so lush. He felt irritated that what she was wearing hid her body completely. Why would a woman so beautiful dress herself in such awful clothes? That drab green trench coat was awful. The black dress underneath looked almost as bad as her chunky black shoes.

The only black Royce liked to see on a woman was in the underwear department, and then only in passing. If she were *his* woman, he'd dress her in a deep red, or emerald-green, or peacock-blue. And he'd adorn those gorgeous slender ankles of hers with the highest, strappiest, sexiest shoes he could find.

Hell, she was leaving!

Not one to be slow off the mark, Royce leapt into action, contriving to bump into the woman as she exited the shop.

'I am so sorry,' he apologised, gripping her elbow to steady her. 'Are you all right?'

'Perfectly, thank you,' she said crisply.

Up close she was even more exquisite, he thought, his desire for her increasing with each second. God, if only they were back in the caveman days... he'd knock her on the head and drag her back to his lair where he wouldn't let her see the light of day for weeks!

'I should have been watching where I was going,' he said, relieved to find that her hands were ringless. He always steered well clear of married women. 'Could I offer you a cup of coffee, perhaps, by way of apology?'

Those incredible black eyes of hers blinked wide as they lifted to his face, fear immediately shooting into their inky depths.

Royce was shocked. What had she seen in his face to make her react like this? He thought he was being all smooth charm; that his carnal intentions were well hidden behind a suitably suave façade.

'No, thank you,' she whispered shakily. 'I . . . I have to go.' And before he could blink, she bolted across the foyer and out through the glass doors, diving into one of the taxis waiting there. She was gone before Royce could gather his wits enough even to note the number and make of the cab.

'Damn,' he muttered, hating to lose, even in something as transitory as a passing fancy.

A passing fancy?

That didn't do justice to the passion that had possessed him on looking into the dark, tempestuous gaze. What he wouldn't give to see them fling wide with ecstasy, not fear!

An idea leapt into his belatedly clearing brain, and, whirling, he strode into Whitmore Opals.

Gemma was standing there, thinking about Melanie's unexpected visit, when someone coughed. Startled, she looked up to find a man on the other side of the counter, a tough-looking man with intense blue eyes and a five o'clock shadow on his chin.

'Excuse me, miss,' he said in a Michael Caine accent. 'That lady you were just talking to. The lady with the black hair. I'm sure I know her. Was she English, by any chance?'

'Melanie? Oh, no, she's Australian. At least, I think she is . . .' Gemma frowned, realising she knew nothing much about Melanie except that she'd been the housekeeper at Belleview for a couple of years, and had an unhappy past, her husband and baby having been killed in a car accident some years ago.

'You mean you know the lady *personally*?' the English tourist was asking.

She smiled at him. 'Yes, I do. She works for my father-in-law.'

'Your father-in-law,' he repeated, giving her an incisive look. 'But you look far too young to be married.'

'Well, married she is,' announced another male voice.

'Nathan!' Gemma exclaimed, delight quickly changing to consternation when she saw how her handsome husband was scowling at the Englishman. Surely he didn't think the man had been flirting with her!

'This is my—er—husband,' she said, feeling flustered with Nathan's display of jealousy. It wasn't the first time he'd made things awkward when he thought a man was paying attention to her. At first, she'd found his possessiveness flattering, but not so much any more.

'Nathan Whitmore,' Nathan said coldly, and held out his hand.

The Englishman shook it. 'How do you do? Royce Grantham.'

'I thought I recognised you,' Nathan remarked, not sounding overly happy about this man's identity. 'So what is the one and only Royce Grantham doing in our small corner of the world?'

Gemma stared hard at the man but was none the wiser. The name and face meant nothing to her. Which wasn't surprising. She'd only begun to appreciate her ignorance of the world at large since she'd started work in this store two months ago. The Regency Hotel was a mecca for celebrities passing through Sydney. They often browsed through Whitmore Opals, the rest of the staff teasing her over how she always failed to recognise them.

'I'm holidaying,' Mr Grantham said. 'I've just arrived in your beautiful city and have been admiring the sights.'

'So I noticed.'

Gemma cringed at her husband's dry tone.

Their visitor, however, was undeterred. 'I saw that magnificent opal in the window and thought I'd come in and ask about it.'

Gemma's eyes flew to the man's. That was a lie. Or, at least, a twisting of the truth. He'd come in primarily to ask about Melanie.

'I'm afraid I won't be here for the auction on the twenty-first,' he went on. 'I take it, Mr Whitmore, that you are the owner of Whitmore Opals?'

'No, I am not.'

When Nathan wasn't forthcoming with further information, Gemma stepped in. 'Whitmore Opals belongs to my husband's father,' she volunteered, her stomach tight with agitation. Why did Nathan have to act like this? She hated it. Thank the lord Mr Grantham didn't seem offended. He looked very tough indeed.

'The father-in-law you mentioned?' he asked, one eyebrow lifting.

'Yes, that's right. Mr Byron Whitmore.'

'And where would I be able to contact him?'

Gemma picked up and handed over one of their business cards which had the head office address and the telephone number listed as well as the two city stores. 'The head office is not far from here,' she told him, hoping the smile mitigated her husband's rudeness. 'Byron should be there till five at least. If he's not in, you could ask to speak to his daughter, Jade, or to a Mr Kyle Armstrong. He's head of marketing.'

The Englishman smiled at her. 'Thank you for all your help, Mrs Whitmore. You've been most kind. Mr Whitmore,' he nodded curtly, and strode from the shop.

Now that Mr Grantham was gone Gemma couldn't look at Nathan. She knew if she did she wouldn't be able to keep the exasperation out of her eyes.

'I thought I'd drop in and take you out for a surprise lunch,' he said, then added drily, 'It looks as though I arrived just in time.'

Now her eyes snapped up. 'And what does that mean?'

Nathan flashed her a frustrated look. 'Just get your coat, Gemma. I don't want to argue with you in front of people.'

Gemma glanced around the store and noticed that a couple of customers were throwing curious glances their way. The rest of the staff were diplomatically ignoring them. Feeling disconcerted, Gemma hurried into the back room where she dragged her coat down from the coatstand and picked up her handbag.

'I'm going to lunch now,' she said as she walked past the other two salesgirls. 'I should be back by two.'

They murmured their assent and soon Nathan was guiding Gemma from the hotel entrance and out into the city street.

'There was no need for you to be so rude to that man, Nathan,' she blurted out at last.

'There was every need,' he bit out, his fingers digging into her arm through the coat. 'I suppose you're going to tell me you don't know who Royce Grantham is.'

'No, I don't. All I know about the gentleman is that he's English.'

'He's no gentleman. Not even remotely.'

'You know him, do you?'

'I've read about him.'

'What is he, then? A movie star or something?'

Nathan's laughter was harsh. '*Or something* just about describes him, I would think. He won the Formula One world championship two years on the trot, and has a reputation for being the most cut-throat ruthless driver that ever drew breath.'

'So? What has that got to do with me, or what happened just now?'

'He also has a reputation for being just as ruthless with women. The man's a predator of the worst kind, and I won't have him hanging around *my wife*.'

Oh, how Gemma was beginning to hate the way Nathan said that! *His* wife. She had a name, didn't she? She was a person, not a possession.

'You've got it all wrong, Nathan,' she sighed. 'He wasn't the slightest bit interested in me. If you must know, he came in to ask about Melanie.'

'*Melanie*?'

'Yes. She'd just been in to show me what she'd bought for Jade and Kyle for an engagement present, and to make sure we hadn't forgotten about the dinner Byron is having for them tonight. Mr Grantham had apparently glimpsed her through the window and thought he knew her.'

'Good God, Gemma, don't you know that's the oldest trick in the book? It's you he wanted to meet. As if a

man would look twice at Melanie when he had someone
as breathtakingly lovely as you in his sight. Lord!'

Nathan ground to a halt and turned Gemma to face
him, his expression reflecting frustration and concern.
'When are you going to realise what this world is really
like, darling? It's rotten through and through, and most
of the people in it.'

Gemma groaned. 'I hate it when you talk like this,
Nathan. I've always believed that most people were good
and I want to keep holding on to that belief. Please don't
try to change me.'

His face softened as love filled his gaze. Now Gemma
melted. When he looked at her like that she forgave him
anything, even his persistent jealousy and world-weary
cynicism. 'As if I would ever want to change you, my
darling,' he whispered, cupping her face and kissing her
gently on the lips. When his mouth lifted, then returned
for a fiercer kiss, she drew back.

'Nathan, we're in the street!'

'So?'

'Do you like embarrassing me?'

'Maybe I like checking that you can still *be* embarrassed,' he said darkly. 'Come on, let's go and have some
lunch and you can tell me what Melanie was doing in
the city anyway. Never known that woman to set foot
outside of Belleview except to visit her brother every
Sunday!'

Melanie paid off the taxi and dashed inside, relieved to
be safely home at Belleview.

That awful man, she thought breathlessly. Trying to
pick me up like that. Did he think she didn't know what
he wanted, or that she hadn't met the likes of him before?

But that wasn't the worst of it. The worst was the way
he'd made *her* feel for one mad moment. As though she
actually wanted to go with him!

Melanie had been struggling to keep that appalling
realisation at bay all the way home in the taxi. And she'd
managed fairly well by concentrating on feelings like
outrage and indignation. But now that she was alone,
she could no longer find the will to deny the truth.

Yes, she'd found him instantly attractive. Yes, she'd been flattered by his obvious pass. Yes, she'd been momentarily tempted to have coffee with him. And maybe more...

Her moan of bewilderment and dismay came from deep within her soul.

She'd been so *sure* no man could ever make her feel like that again, so sure that that part of her life was dead, as her husband and baby were dead. After what happened with Joel, she wanted to have nothing more to do with men and, quite frankly, there hadn't been one incident in the past few years to shake her belief that she would live the rest of her life in a sexless void.

Till today...

A memory of the man's ruggedly handsome face and hard, sexy blue eyes flashed into her mind and she shuddered. Maybe it was the one-off thing, came the clutched-at hope, an aberration never to be repeated. If it was, then she was safe. After all, she would never see him again. Sydney had four million people in it and, given her tendency to leave Belleview only rarely, the odds of running into that individual again were not worth worrying about. Besides, he had sounded English. No doubt he was a tourist, just passing through.

Her logical thoughts having soothed her near panic, Melanie levered herself away from the front door to make her way shakily across the wide marble foyer. But as she passed the huge Italian gilt mirror that hung on the wall, her reflection halted her, a gasp of shock flying from her lips.

Was that her, that flushed impassioned-looking creature with pink cheeks and eyes like glittering black coals?

A cry of torment flew from her lips and she dropped her handbag on the marble console beneath the mirror, leaning on both with white-knuckled intensity.

'Melanie! Are you all right?'

Gathering herself with great difficulty, Melanie sought for the impassive face she usually found comfort behind, but it took its time in coming. Only by the greatest effort of will did she turn a composed face to the plump woman sweeping down the marble staircase.

'It's that time of the month, I'm afraid,' she lied valiantly. 'I'll be fine in an hour or two.'

'You shouldn't have gone out shopping,' Ava said kindly. 'I could have bought whatever it was you had to buy. Oops...'

Melanie froze when Ava's foot slipped on the bottom step and she almost went flying. Luckily, she was able to grab the corner of the balustrade to right herself and Melanie heaved a ragged sigh of relief. Thirtyish and overweight, Ava Whitmore was the most accident-prone person she had ever known. Hardly a day went by without her either falling over, or crashing into someone, or breaking something.

Melanie felt sorry for her employer's younger and only sister. What sort of life did she have, spending all her days painting watercolour landscapes that she never finished, then filling her evenings watching endless movies on television or video? Ava had never had a real job or a real boyfriend in her life. Apparently, Byron had routed a few males of the gold-digging variety in her earlier days, leaving the woman with little self-esteem and a tendency to cocoon herself from real life.

Yet she was a warm, motherly woman with a lot to offer the right man. Not bad-looking either, with lovely blue eyes and a pretty mouth. All she needed to look presentable was to lose a few pounds and get that awful ginger hair dyed back to its original brown.

Melanie found it ironic that she would want for Ava what bitter experience told her was a hazardous path to happiness. Wasn't Ava's self-imposed seclusion a safer option to her going forth into the world and putting her future into the hands of a member of the opposite sex? Melanie was not nearly as vulnerable a type as Ava, yet the man *she'd* trusted and loved had ultimately destroyed her life, along with her capacity either to trust or to love a man ever again.

She'd thought Joel had also destroyed her capacity to respond in *any* way to a man again. But it seemed she'd been wrong about that, she realised with a shudder of self-disgust.

'I think you should come with me to the kitchen,' Ava suggested, taking her elbow with uncharacteristic firmness, 'where you can sit down while I make you a cup of tea.'

Melanie gave in gracefully and was soon seated at the breakfast bar while Ava busied herself making the tea, during which activity she first spilt the sugar, then dropped a mug which, luckily, didn't break.

'I must have the dropsy today,' she said breathlessly.

Finally, the tea was safely made and Ava hoisted herself up on to a stool to devour her own, along with several chocolate biscuits. Melanie wished she wouldn't eat so many sweet things, but didn't say anything.

'What do you think of Jade and Kyle Armstrong becoming engaged so quickly?' she said instead. 'Not to mention her moving in with him.'

Ava shrugged. 'Young people don't know how to wait for things these days. Still... I would never begrudge Jade any happiness. She's had a hard time of it lately, what with her mother dying in that boating accident and all.'

'That's true,' was Melanie's non-committal remark.

Privately, she thought Jade was better off without her mother, who'd been an atrocious neurotic who'd thankfully spent more time in sanatoriums than home with her husband and daughter at Belleview. She'd been in one such place when Melanie had originally accepted the position as Byron's housekeeper. She might not have come to Belleview at all if Mrs Whitmore had been in residence at the time, for it had infuriated Melanie to watch a mother being so emotionally abusive of her daughter. Didn't she know how lucky she was to *have* a child? Luckily, Jade was a girl of some spirit. A more timid person would have withered under Irene Whitmore's constant criticism and sarcasm.

As for Jade's father...Byron Whitmore was a patriarch of the old-fashioned type, overbearing, bossy and chauvinistic. Clearly, he'd found his daughter's rebellious teenage years a bewildering experience, failing to understand what lay behind her outrageous escapades. From what Melanie herself had witnessed, Irene had been very clever and sly in her parental tyranny and Byron never saw first-hand what his daughter had to put up with. It was no wonder the girl had sought love outside the home. She'd received little enough within its walls.

Jade deserved a break in Melanie's opinion, and the break had come along in the guise of Kyle Armstrong. The new marketing manager for Whitmore Opals was just what the girl needed, a strong hand and a loving heart. Best of all, he seemed to have cured the girl of her one-time infatuation for Nathan, who was not the man for any young girl.

Which brought Melanie to think about Nathan's recent marriage to Gemma.

She frowned. From the moment Nathan had brought Gemma home to Belleview a few months ago, it had been obvious the girl was smitten with him. And why not? Nathan was incredibly handsome in the golden-boy style of a young Robert Redford. At only twenty and country-naïve, Gemma was no match for a thirty-five-year-old sophisticate hell bent on sampling her glorious innocence.

What Melanie—and quite a few others—had not expected was that Nathan would marry the girl. His ex-wife had been as stunned by the union as everyone else, because Nathan had vowed never to remarry, his divorce only having come through two years ago. His daughter Kirsty had been very upset, because she'd hoped that her parents would ultimately reconcile. A foolish hope, given that the pair had never been in love. Or so Ava had told Melanie when Lenore and Nathan had called their marriage quits some time back.

'I'd give Kyle's and Jade's marriage a far better chance of success than Nathan and Gemma's,' Ava suddenly said, as though her mind had been going along the same track as Melanie's.

'I have to agree with you on the age-difference alone,' Melanie commented. 'Fifteen years as opposed to what? Six or seven? How old is Kyle, exactly?'

'Twenty-eight, I think.'

'Still,' Melanie mused, 'Gemma seemed happy enough when I saw her in town today.'

'It's only been a few weeks. Wait till the honeymoon wears off and Nathan shows his true colours.'

Ava's tartness surprised Melanie. Was it possible she had once been infatuated with Nathan herself? Though herself immune to his brand of sex appeal, Melanie had seen it in action plenty of times. Yet as a person he remained an enigma to her. What lay behind the cool glamorous mask he wore? What kind of man was he really?

'Tell me about Nathan, Ava,' she asked carefully, sipping her tea in a casual fashion. 'He was only sixteen when Byron adopted him, wasn't he?'

'He'd turned seventeen by then,' the older woman corrected, an acid tone in her voice. 'Seventeen, going on thirty. Understandable, considering the kind of life he was living.'

'What kind of life was that?'

'The kind a lot of street kids fall into up at the Cross, I suppose. Living off his wits. *And* his body.'

Melanie sat bolt upright. 'Are you saying Nathan prostituted himself?'

Ava shrugged. 'Not exactly. But I overheard Byron telling Irene about finding him living with a woman of forty! If that's not a form of prostitution I don't know what is!'

'But he was only a boy then, Ava. If that was what was going on, surely the woman was the one to blame, not Nathan! Besides, I can't see Byron bringing anyone basically bad into his home.'

'My brother can be very blind sometimes. All he would have seen was a boy in need, a soul in danger of being lost, and he would have been compelled to save him. To give him credit, Nathan has done Byron proud in most respects. He worked hard to learn the opal business and his plays have taken the world by storm. Though God knows why. I think they're over the top.'

'I've never seen one. What's over the top about them?'

'The way the characters behave. They're so emotional in a frightening, out-of-control way. The stories are cruel and violent as well. His plays don't entertain you. They disturb you. I only went to one and one was enough, thank you.'

'Yet Nathan is a very controlled person himself,' Melanie murmured thoughtfully.

'Yes. Odd, isn't it?'

'Maybe...'

Ava sighed. 'He's a puzzle all right, I'll give you that. Still, he's always been a good father to Kirsty and at least he did marry Gemma. Though I wonder if he only did that because of Byron.'

'Why because of Byron?'

'You know what a stickler Byron is for doing the right thing, and Nathan does like to keep in Byron's good books. Byron thinks the sun shines out of him. Of course, there have been certain incidents with certain females in the past that Byron never saw and which I for one would never enlighten him on. But who knows? Maybe I'm wrong. Maybe Nathan's changed. Maybe he genuinely loves Gemma. We can only hope, I suppose. But, as they say, leopards don't change their spots.'

A pensive silence developed, broken when the telephone on the kitchen wall rang.

'I'll get it,' Melanie said immediately, fearful that any hurried movement of Ava's might result in another accident.

'Belleview,' she answered.

'Byron here, Melanie. There'll be another person for dinner tonight. A gentleman. I hope that will be all right.'

'Yes, of course.'

'Sorry to give you such late notice. Must go. I have some important business to finish up and I don't want to be late home.'

The line went dead and Melanie rolled her eyes.

'What is it?' Ava asked. 'Is there anything wrong?'

'No. Just Byron adding another head to the dinner party tonight.'

'Oh? Who?'

'I don't know. A gentleman. Look, if I don't get a move on there won't be *any* dinner party tonight. At least, not one with food.'

'Can I help?'

'Oh—er—no, I don't think so, but thanks for offering. Rita will be here later to set the table and help serve. You go and make yourself pretty. Who knows? The gentleman Byron's bringing home might be an eligible bachelor.'

'Even if he is, he won't look at the likes of me,' Ava said bleakly.

'Don't sell yourself short, Ava. You've got a lot to offer a man.'

'Only my money.'

'That's not true. You're an attractive woman.'

'I'm too fat. Most men only want slim and sensational.'

'More fool them.'

Ava was startled by the bitter tone in Melanie's voice. She had never heard the other woman sound so vehement. Come to think of it, Melanie wasn't her usual self today. She seemed . . . agitated. And it had nothing to do with the time of the month. Something had happened during her shopping trip, something that had upset her.

Ava wished she could ask her about it but Melanie might think she was prying. Byron's housekeeper was a very private person who kept her own counsel and clearly liked it that way. Ava sighed and slipped from her stool, her heavy landing reminding her of her weight.

No man is ever going to look at me, she thought wearily. Why I bothered to go and buy that new outfit I have no idea. Still, I might as well go and try to make a silk purse out of a sow's ear. I've got nothing else to do.

CHAPTER TWO

By SIX-THIRTY that evening Melanie was grateful she'd chosen a menu which was deceptively easy to prepare, because, where Ava had had dropsy earlier, *she* had now developed a severe case of distraction.

The reason did not elude her. It was crystal-clear. Irritatingly so. She could not get the incident with that man out of her mind.

'Damn him,' she muttered, banging the cutlery drawer shut.

'I hope you're not talking about me.'

Melanie swung round as her employer strode into the kitchen from the direction of the garages.

'You're home early for a Friday,' she said, side-stepping Byron's comment.

'I wanted to be showered and changed by the time Royce arrived. I told him seven, which means if he's on time I'll have him to myself for a while. The others aren't due till seven-thirty.' He was taking off his tie as he hurried through the room. 'Make sure both ice-buckets in the drawing-room are full, will you, Melanie?'

Byron was gone before she could do more than draw breath. Ever since his shattered leg had finally mended, he'd been a whirlwind of energy, his mind going as fast as his body. Though fifty next birthday, he was by no means middle-aged, either in looks or manner. An exceptionally handsome man, with thick wavy black hair, elegantly grey at the temples, he propelled his impressively proportioned body around with a dynamism that a man twenty years his junior would envy.

A thought suddenly crossed Melanie's mind.

I wonder what Byron does for sex these days?

Instant irritation sent her winged black brows drawing together. There she was again, thinking thoughts that wouldn't normally occur to her these days! It was all that damned man's fault. Him and his sleazy looks and filthy desires.

Filthy?

Now Melanie brought herself up short. She'd never been one of those women who'd thought sex dirty or filthy. She'd always enjoyed making love, even those first nervous attempts with her high-school sweetheart.

A smile of wry remembrance pulled at her generous mouth. What a hopeless pair they had been! His name had been Grant, and he'd been rather sweet and shy, even at eighteen. They'd been going together for a couple of years before he'd drummed up the courage to ask her to go all the way. His lovemaking had been very basic and fumbling, and, while Melanie could not say she'd ever seen stars, she had loved the feel of his hands on her body, loved the warmth and intimacy of it all.

Grant had lasted all during her year at secretarial college, right up till she secured a job as a secretary-receptionist for Eagles Advertising Agency, an American company with a highly successful branch in Sydney. There, she'd caught the eye of an up-and-coming advertising executive named Joel Lloyd. From the moment Joel Lloyd decided Melanie Foster was the woman for him, poor Grant didn't stand a chance.

A bitter taste invaded Melanie's mouth as she thought of the difference between her two lovers. Two years it had taken Grant to work up the courage to consummate their relationship. Joel had seduced her in the company store-room two weeks after they'd been introduced. And she'd very definitely seen stars!

But that had been typical of Joel. He was one of those men who took risks, who dared while other men dithered. He'd been a ruthless man, there was no doubt about that. What a shame she hadn't realised right from the start just how ruthless he was, then maybe her baby would still be alive...

Melanie shuddered before giving herself a mental shake. I'm not going to think about the past any more. If I do, I'll go mad. I'm going to concentrate on the here and now of my life, which is that all of a sudden a man has sparked an unexpected and unwanted sexual response in me. With a bit of luck, that spark will snuff out again, quite quickly. I'm certainly going to work on it, because sex can make a woman vulnerable to a man, and I am never going to be vulnerable to a man again. Never ever!

Melanie set about the final preparations for the evening meal, annoyed to find that her train of thought had made her uncomfortably aware of her woman's body beneath her simple black skirt and white blouse. Her breasts felt tight against her bra, and when she walked she was conscious of her stockings brushing together at the tops of her thighs. God, but it was proving hard to concentrate on doing even the simplest task.

What a pity that tonight of all nights Rita couldn't come to lend a hand. Rita's teenage son had come down with the chicken pox and with her husband not due home from work till late she felt she had to stay home. Melanie could have rung round the assortment of casual helpers she had on her books, but that would have taken as long as just doing it all herself. Normally, she could have handled a dinner party for seven standing on her head, but tonight she was not her usual efficient self.

Now what was it Byron had asked her to do? Oh, yes, the ice-buckets in the drawing-room. Melanie hurried to collect the buckets and was filling them with ice-cubes from the freezer when the front doorbell rang. The clock on the wall said five to seven, which meant Byron's special guest was early—a most uncommon occurrence these days. Muttering, Melanie sped back to the drawing-room, replaced the buckets in the drinks cabinet and dashed to answer the door, smoothing any stray hairs back behind her ears as she went.

Feeling quite harried, she couldn't even drum up a polite smile as she opened the door.

Even if she had, it would have been frozen on her face.

'You!' she exclaimed, black eyes rounding. 'What...
what are you doing here?' she cried, quickly followed
by an outraged, 'How dare you follow me?'

Too late it occurred to Melanie that the unwanted per-
sonage on the front doorstep was wearing a dinner suit.
This afternoon he'd been dressed in faded blue jeans
and a brown leather jacket. Would a would-be pursuer
put on formal dress simply to chase after a female prey?
And would he have waited till evening to knock at her
door? Not very likely.

Reality returned with crashing embarrassment.

'You're Byron's extra guest,' she realised aloud,
groaning silently. This was fate at its most wicked! 'Royce
Something-or-other,' she added in a raw whisper.

To her mortification, he laughed. 'That's me all right.
Royce Something-or-other.'

Her temper rose at his obvious amusement, and she
had to fight for composure. 'Byron didn't tell me your
full name,' she said agitatedly.

'He didn't tell me yours, either. Melanie what?'

Those sharp blue eyes locked on to hers and in that
moment it came to her in a swamping wave of shock
that she'd been right the first time. He *had* followed her.
Somehow. This was no fickle finger of fate. This was
man at his most dangerous and predatory. She didn't
know how he'd found out where she lived or how he'd
wangled an invitation to dinner tonight, but she knew,
without a shadow of a doubt, that he had. He was
another Joel, this Royce Something-or-other. She recognised the type as forcefully as her subconscious had
recognised it earlier in the day.

Unfortunately, she still seemed to find this type in-
sidiously attractive.

Her breath caught in her throat as her eyes swept over
him once more. The dinner suit lent an urbane elegance
to his hard lean body. His thatch of thick straight brown
hair had been tamed with some gel and swept back from
his forehead. The five o'clock shadow he'd been sporting
earlier in the day was gone, replaced by an aftershave
that was fresh and tangy. But despite his superb grooming

there was still something uncivilised about him which made her heart leap and her senses spring to attention.

It was his eyes, she realised, that gave him away. For their expressive blue depths were the windows to his soul. And his soul was the soul of a dark and dangerous man, a man who didn't know how to lose. Oh, yes, she recognised the type, only too well.

But forewarned was forearmed and be damned if she would let him know her susceptibility to such men.

'My name is Melanie Lloyd,' she said coolly. 'I am the housekeeper here at Belleview. I am thirty-two years old and a widow. I do not date. *Ever.* Do I make myself clear, Mr Royce Something-or-other?'

'Perfectly. For the record, my name is Royce Grantham. I am thirty-six. Single. And I do date. A lot. On top of that I think you are the most exquisitely beautiful woman I have ever seen.'

Her mocking smile would have put off most men, as would the acid tone of her words. 'How very original of you, Mr Grantham. Do come in. Byron is looking forward to your no doubt entertaining company. But might I give you a word of warning? He's not a man who likes flattery so try not to indulge your obvious tendency for flamboyant exaggeration.'

'You know Byron well, do you?' his guest drawled as he followed the wave of her hand inside.

For a second Melanie's nostrils flared, her eyes flashing with fury at the implication behind his words. But she refused to give this horrid creature the satisfaction of an angry retort. Gathering herself, she dredged up one of her frostiest faces and turned its chill upon him full blast. 'I've been Mr Whitmore's housekeeper for two years, during which time I have come to appreciate the genuine gentleman he is. Now if you will come this way, Mr Grantham, I'll settle you in the drawing-room and find out what is keeping your host.'

Melanie was sure she didn't breathe till she left the drawing-room. Her head was whirling and she had to stop on the first step of the staircase to pull herself together. Their visitor had not said another personal word to her, but she had felt the magnetic pull of his eyes, even as she left the room.

Why he should be interested in her as he so obviously was, amazed her. She'd long passed the days when her looks had stopped men in their tracks. Oh, yes, there had been a time, in the early years of her marriage to Joel, when that had happened. Joel had been a man of great sophistication and taste, and known exactly how to make her over from the pretty teenager he had married into a very striking woman. He'd dressed her in vivid colours, and in simple but daring styles which more often than not required a minimum of underwear. And of course her long black hair had always been worn loose then.

But Melanie was under no illusion about her appearance these days. She mostly wore black and in unbecoming styles. She used no make-up and her hair was always pulled back in a severe knot or roll. If that wasn't enough to deter a man, her aloof manner usually polished off any burgeoning interest.

Yet something—some perverse appeal—had made this man fancy her enough to pursue her. And he didn't mean to give up. If Melanie knew anything about this type of male, it was the stubbornness of his ego. He would be merciless in the chase. And bold.

It was the boldness that bothered her the most.

Because boldness had once excited her. Very much.

'Did I hear the doorbell ring just now?'

Melanie glanced up to see Byron hurrying down the stairs towards her. Also dressed in black dinner suit, he was much more traditionally handsome than the man seated in the brocade armchair in the drawing-room. Why didn't Byron excite her? Why didn't *his* sexy blue eyes send her blood racing?

'Melanie?' Byron stopped to touch her on the shoulder, concern on his face. 'Are you all right, my dear?'

She stiffened under his touch, for it left her cold, as his eyes left her cold.

Her covering smile was born of panic, for she couldn't bear for Byron to get a hint of what was troubling her. 'Sorry. Just wool-gathering. Yes, that was the doorbell. I put your Mr Grantham in the drawing-room. He said he'd wait for you to join him before he had a drink.'

'Good.' Byron reached up to give his black bowtie a last straightening. 'So what did you think of the famous Royce Grantham, eh, Melanie?'

'Famous?' she repeated blankly.

'You mean you don't know who he is?' Byron seemed amused. 'Isn't that just like a woman? I'll bet Ava doesn't recognise him, either. Royce Grantham happens to have won the Formula One world championship not once, but twice! He retired at the height of his career a couple of years back.'

'What's he doing here?' Melanie asked, her throat dry.

'He's passing through Sydney on a world tour and staying at the Regency. Apparently he's become quite a collector during his travels, and when he saw our Heart of Fire opal in the hotel shop he came to see me, thinking he could persuade me to sell it to him before the auction. He's got Buckley's, I'm afraid. But he insisted on a further chance to persuade me so I invited him along tonight. Who knows? Maybe we'll be able to get him to buy some of our other opals instead. He's damned rich enough to afford a swag.'

Byron moved on, leaving Melanie to stare after him with a sinking feeling in her stomach. A world champion racing driver... She should have guessed he'd be something like that. A risk-taker of the first order. A thrill-seeker extraordinaire. A raving lunatic!

When her heart began to beat even faster, she groaned anew. Turning, she fled back to her kitchen, determined to hide there till circumstances forced her to leave.

The first circumstance was the front doorbell ringing at twenty to eight. Muttering to herself, she hurried to answer it, meeting a nervous-looking Ava in the foyer. Melanie was taken aback to see the other woman wearing a surprisingly elegant royal-blue silk trouser suit whose simple long-line jacket and loose-legged trousers hid her plumpness very well.

'My, don't you look nice!' she complimented warmly. 'That's new, isn't it?'

Ava flushed with pleasure. 'You really like it? I bought it at a boutique Lenore told me about which specialises in making big women look better. I'm thinking I might go back and splurge on some more outfits.'

'Why don't you? That one looks great.'

The doorbell rang again.

'Do you think that's Byron's gentleman guest?' Ava whispered, looking a little more confident now.

Melanie's insides contracted at this reminder of Royce Grantham. 'No, he arrived half an hour ago.'

'He did? Goodness, he was early. What's he like? Don't tell me he's an old fogy!'

'Hardly. He's one of those crazy Formula One racing drivers,' Melanie bit out. 'Byron says he was once world champion.'

Ava's eyes lit up. 'You mean he's Italian?'

Quite clearly, Italian men figured largely in Ava's romantic fantasies. 'Sorry. British. A Mr Royce Grantham. I must answer the door, Ava,' she excused herself. 'Why don't you go along to the drawing-room? Byron and Mr Grantham are having pre-dinner drinks in there.'

'I think I'll wait and go along with whoever is arriving.'

Melanie opened the door to find both couples standing there, waiting. Nathan and Gemma. Kyle and Jade.

What a striking foursome they were, she thought: Nathan, coolly resplendent in a white dinner-jacket; Gemma, lush in wine-coloured velvet; Kyle, wickedly handsome in black and Jade, dazzling in a red wool dress that showed every curve of her spectacular figure.

Melanie began to appreciate how Ava must feel sometimes, having to compete with her glamorous family, though at least tonight Byron's sister could hold her own. She really did look very attractive in that blue. Melanie's compliment seemed to have done wonders for her confidence as well, for she came sashaying forwards without putting a foot wrong and proceeded to shower everyone with warm kisses, adding hearty congratulations to the newly engaged Kyle and Jade.

Melanie extended her own best wishes as she hung up various overcoats, and, when she got the chance, drew Jade over to the console in the hall where she had placed the present she had bought them earlier that evening.

'I saw this and couldn't resist,' she explained on handing the prettily wrapped package to a startled Jade.

'Oh, how kind of you! Wasn't it kind of Melanie, darling, to buy us a gift?' she directed at Kyle, who joined them, smiling.

'Very kind,' he agreed.

Melanie was pleased that both of them seemed to genuinely like her present—an antique photograph frame made in real silver, with a scrolly edge that was both intricate and romantic-looking.

'I thought you could put one of your wedding photographs in it,' she suggested. 'When is the big day to be? Have you set a date yet?'

Jade flashed her fiancé a surprisingly coy look. 'Soon, I think,' she murmured.

'Very soon,' Kyle insisted.

Jade laughed, her eyes still on the man she loved. 'Perhaps we'll elope, like Nathan and Gemma here.'

'I think Byron might appreciate the privilege of giving his only daughter away, don't you?' Kyle advised gently.

'Speaking of Byron,' Ava piped up, 'you'll never guess who he has in the drawing-room.' She glanced around the group, looking and sounding like a little girl, dying to tell a secret.

'You're quite right, Ava,' Nathan said drily. 'We couldn't guess, so just tell us. But if you say Celeste Campbell then I for one won't believe you.'

'Neither will I,' Jade laughed.

Now if there was one thing Melanie would have liked to find out about her employer it was what lay behind the feud between him and Celeste Campbell. But she doubted she ever would. Byron's hatred of his half-sister-in-law and main business rival was only exceeded by his reluctance ever to discuss her. She was *verboten* in this household!

'Don't be ridiculous, you two,' Ava said reproachfully. 'Hell will freeze over before Byron invites Celeste Campbell to Belleview. No, it's Royce Grantham. You know...the champion British racing car driver!'

'*Really*?' Jade exclaimed, the only one of the foursome to look pleased by the news. Kyle was frowning, and Nathan exchanged a glance with Gemma that bespoke more than a passing irritation at the news of an additional guest. Privately, Melanie agreed that Byron shouldn't have imposed a virtual stranger—no matter who or what he was—on what was essentially a family occasion. But Byron was not large on sensitivity. Unfortunately.

Oblivious of the sudden atmosphere, Jade breezed forward and slipped an arm through Ava's elbow. 'I've read about him. He's supposed to be a one with the ladies, if I recall. You'd better watch yourself, Auntie. You're looking rather scrumptious tonight in that blue suit. Have you been on a diet?'

'Not really.'

'Well, you're looking fab, so I'm going to stay close and ward off Mr Grantham's passes. Or do you want him to make passes? Yes, of course you do. How silly of me!' She was off and propelling Ava down to the drawing-room before any of the others could stop her. Nathan urged Gemma after them, Kyle dragging the chain, his frown deep and dark.

Melanie could only assume that Kyle had met Royce at Whitmore Opals head office today, and either didn't like him, or didn't like his trying to persuade Byron to sell the Heart of Fire before the ball. Why else would he be perturbed by the Englishman's presence? It wasn't as though Jade was upset by her father's inviting an extra guest, even if Nathan was.

Whatever, it seemed Melanie wasn't the only person who didn't want Royce Grantham's presence here this evening. Still, not wanting him here wasn't going to change anything. He *was* here. Neither could she do what she would dearly love to do, which was vanish herself for the next few hours. She had to serve dinner, from the hors-d'oeuvres to the last cup of coffee. All she could do to cope was hide her agitation behind a coolly controlled façade.

Everyone else would probably think she was in one of her remote moods. But tonight, it would all be acting. Melanie felt far from remote when she thought about being in the same room as Royce Grantham. And far from coolly controlled.

CHAPTER THREE

GEMMA couldn't believe it!

Nathan could, of course.

Even as they'd been driving through the gates of Belleview a few minutes before, he'd made another pointed remark about her naïveté over men. She'd scorned his opinion that Royce Grantham would show up to bother her again, and what happened? Her supposed admirer turned up here as a dinner guest tonight.

Coincidence was impossible. That infernal man had deliberately wangled an invitation from Byron so that he could see Melanie again. But since Nathan hadn't believed her assertion the first time that it was Byron's housekeeper the Englishman was interested in, then he wasn't going to the second time either.

Even if Royce Grantham *had* taken a fancy to her, Gemma would still have been upset with Nathan's attitude. It took two to tango, didn't it? Where was his faith in her love, his trust? Did he honestly believe she would go off with some stranger? She loved Nathan to death and no other man interested her. Yet her husband was looking daggers at her as they traipsed after Jade and Ava. Anyone would think, by the expression in his eyes, that she had planned this all herself!

'Ah, there you are,' Byron boomed as they entered the drawing-room. 'Come and meet Royce. I'm sure the men will recognise him, if not the ladies.'

Gemma, for one, almost didn't. *Again.* What had the man done to himself since lunchtime? Where had the rough and tough image disappeared to?

In its place was a suave, elegant, almost handsome creature who looked like he'd stepped out of one of those fashion magazines. His black dinner suit fitted like a

glove, its satin lapels as sleek and shiny as his hair.
Amazing!

She stiffened as those sharp blue eyes of his started
running over the group, seemingly searching for something—or someone.

Melanie, Gemma hoped, and held her breath. She
couldn't help sighing with relief when his gaze slid right
over her without stopping, a fact which Nathan couldn't
have failed to notice.

'Clever bastard,' Nathan muttered in her ear. 'He
doesn't want to look obvious.'

Gemma could have screamed. Only by clenching her
teeth hard in her jaw did she stop her frustration from
finding voice. Better not to say anything, she decided.
Arguing with irrational people was a waste of time.

A disturbing thought jumped into her mind as she
stood there, seething silently. This was exactly the tack
she'd been forced to use with her father in the weeks
leading up to his death. For some reason, after she left
school, he'd become extra paranoid and possessive about
her, refusing to let her leave Lightning Ridge to find
work, and often losing his temper if she was five minutes
late home. At first she'd stood up to him, but when he
retaliated with violence she'd begun to handle his irrational outbursts with silence. And while this was
physically safer, she'd hated the triumph in his eyes when
he thought she'd been cowed into submission.

Gemma slid a frowning glance up at her husband.
Surely her relationship with Nathan wasn't going to de-
velop the same minefields as her relationship with her
father? She didn't want to have to tippy-toe around his
moods for fear of potential outbursts, didn't want to
feel she couldn't *talk* to him, couldn't discuss things in
a sane, logical fashion.

Once again, she was struck by how little they did actually talk. This lack of communication had raised its
ugly head on their honeymoon at Avoca, but she hadn't
noticed it so much since they'd returned to Sydney to
live and she'd started working. Maybe she'd been too
busy. True, Nathan did make an effort to stop his writing

as soon as she came home of an evening, but more often than not they went out—first to dinner and then to the theatre or a movie. It was hard to have meaningful chit-chat in a restaurant, or in a crowded theatre. Then, when they finally returned to the flat, Nathan would take her to bed and make beautiful love to her, after which he would promptly fall asleep.

Still, most women would have thought Gemma had it made. She lived in a glamorous unit overlooking Elizabeth Bay, had a glamorous job working in a ritzy opal store, wore glamorous clothes which cost more than most people earned in a year, and had a glamorous husband who was mad about her. In a way, she felt impatient with herself. What more did she want?

The answer was crystal-clear. To have a truly close relationship with her husband, where they knew and understood each other deeply, intimately, where their love was expressed in other ways besides sexually, where she was his friend and confidante, not just his lover.

Gemma dragged herself back to the present to hear Nathan explaining to Byron that they had already met Mr Grantham earlier that day.

'Really? Where?'

'At the Regency shop.'

'Ah, yes, of course. Royce said he'd been there, looking at the Heart of Fire. But what were you doing there, Nathan? I thought you were well into a new play.'

Nathan shrugged. 'I've had to put it aside for a while. It's not working out.'

'In that case you should consider my other offer.'

'What other offer?' Gemma joined in, frowning. Why hadn't he told *her* his writing wasn't going well?

'I'm having trouble finding the right director for the play of Nathan's that I'm producing. I've asked Nathan to consider doing it himself. He'd be perfect. Still, we'll talk about that later. Jade, come over here. Kyle, where are you? Why are you lurking back there near the door? Come and join Jade so that we can finish these introductions and then break open the champagne to toast your engagement.'

Kyle came forward, a wry smile on his face. 'Mr Grantham and I are also previously acquainted,' he said, slipping an arm around Jade's waist and kissing her on the cheek. 'There's nothing for it, darling. We'll have to tell everyone the truth before your father's guest lets the cat out of the bag.'

'The truth?' Ava said, blue eyes blinking wide with curiosity. 'What truth?'

Kyle cleared his throat. 'My last name is not Armstrong, but Gainsford. I've been going under an alias since coming to live here in Sydney.'

Byron was truly taken aback, an angry flush slanting across his high cheekbones. 'Why the devil would you do that? God, you're not some kind of con-man, are you?'

Royce's dry chuckle sent everyone's eyes his way. 'I wouldn't worry about your future son-in-law, Byron, if I were you. The reason Kyle and I know each other is because he was one of my financial backers during my last years on the track. I suspect he could buy you and me both out and still have the odd billion or two left over.'

This news brought an assortment of gasps and stares, plus a mischievous giggle from Jade. 'See the trouble you've got yourself into?' she told her fiancé. 'I told you we should have told everyone before, but no, you said you were enjoying your anonymity too much. Next time you'll listen to me, won't you? Ah, here's Melanie with some much needed refreshments. I think we need something to pop into all the goldfish mouths around the room. Melanie, did you hear Kyle's little confession? Ah, yes, I can see by the look on your face that you did. Well, go on, darling,' she went on, jabbing Kyle in the ribs. 'Trot out the reason behind your deception. Truly, everyone, it's better than Zorro. I haven't heard it nearly often enough yet. It's so wonderfully romantic. And then, when you've finished, we'll drop our other bomb-shell, shall we?'

Kyle groaned. 'I can see there'll be no stopping you.'

'There never has been any stopping my daughter,' Byron said drily.

'You're right about that Byron,' Kyle agreed, giving Jade a look of such love and approval and understanding that Gemma's heart turned over. If only Nathan would look at *her* like that. Passion was all very well, but sometimes it wasn't enough.

'If you don't tell us the story soon, Kyle,' Ava spluttered, 'I'm going to explode!'

'I'm rather curious myself,' Mr Grantham said, amusement glittering in those expressive blue eyes of his.

Kyle sighed. 'This will probably sound hopelessly sentimental and melodramatic, but here goes. The fact is...I've always found my inherited fortune a huge barrier when it came to relationships. It brought me plenty of attention from the opposite sex, but experience gradually taught me that it was very difficult for a man as rich as myself to find a woman to truly love him. I was reaching the age where I wanted to marry and have a family, so I decided to move interstate and assume a false identity where I could look for a wife as an ordinary chap with an ordinary job. I knew Jade was the girl for me the first day I saw her, and luckily she felt the same.'

'I always thought there was something fishy about you,' Nathan said with an ironic chuckle.

'Well, I didn't!' Byron muttered crossly.

'I'm sorry I had to deceive you, Byron,' Kyle went on. 'But I've tried to do a good job at Whitmore's and I'd like to continue as head of marketing. To be honest I'm enjoying the challenge. There's no need for my secret to go any further than this room for a while yet, is there? Jade and I plan to have a very private garden wedding with only her immediate family present so there shouldn't be any problem with publicity.'

'But what about your family, Kyle?' Gemma asked. 'Don't you want to invite them to your wedding?'

'I don't have any family here in Australia. My parents were killed in a bush fire when I was only a tot. I am...' he smiled down at his fiancée '... the classic poor little rich boy who's been lucky enough to find a woman who loves him for himself.'

'And who's going to have his baby,' Jade murmured before throwing her father a slightly worried look.

She needn't have worried. Byron's initial shock soon gave way to a wide beam of delight. 'A baby! My first grandchild! How wonderful!' He came forward to hug his daughter and shake Kyle's hand. 'The wedding will be soon, I hope.'

'As soon as it can be arranged.'

'Well, this does call for champagne. Lucky we put a *couple* of bottles on ice, eh, Royce? We have two reasons to celebrate now. What a night this has turned out to be!'

Amen to that, Melanie thought ruefully as she moved around the room, serving a silver tray of hors-d'oeuvres while Byron and Royce handed out glasses of champagne. She lingered with Nathan and Gemma, exchanging pleasantries, then chatting to Jade till she saw that Royce had moved away to take a glass of champagne to Ava. Melanie filled in a little more time telling Byron about Rita's inability to help tonight, but finally had no option but to approach the enemy. By this time, he was standing in front of the fire, leaning a casual elbow on the mantelpiece while he sipped champagne and listened attentively to a highly animated Ava.

'I really shouldn't,' Ava murmured when presented with the tray.

'I don't see why not,' her companion said, managing to bestow a charming smile upon her while his eyes were all for Melanie. Her black gaze bored back into his, conveying an icy contempt for what he was doing, bewitching poor Ava while secretly lusting after the household help.

Did he think such tactics would make her jealous? He had a lot to learn about Melanie Lloyd if he thought he could manipulate her. Oh, he could set her heart beating with those sexy eyes and that hard virile body of his but never would she let him know it. She'd rather die than give a man—especially a carbon copy of Joel—the slightest power over her again.

'Will you stay and have a glass of champagne with us, Melanie?' Ava asked innocently.

'Can't, I'm afraid, Ava. Rita couldn't make it tonight so I'm all alone in the kitchen.'

'I'm pretty good in a kitchen,' Royce drawled. 'Want a hand?'

'Thank you for the kind offer,' she said with false sweetness, 'but I'm sure Byron wouldn't appreciate a dinner guest spending the evening in his kitchen.'

Her smile was pure acid before she turned away, having decided to leave the food behind as self-serve and escape this corrupter's presence post-haste. But when she bent over to lower the tray on to the nearby coffee-table, her straight black skirt rode up slightly at the back of her legs, as well as pulled tight across her hips and buttocks. Despite her back being to Royce, the hairs on the nape of her neck suddenly stood up on end and she just knew he was watching her intently, not only watching her but undressing her with his eyes.

Appalled at the persistent sexual nature of her thoughts—not to mention the undeniable heat coursing through her veins—she swiftly straightened, wiping sweaty palms down the sides of her skirt. 'When do you want me to serve dinner, Byron?' she asked, amazed to hear that her voice sounded steady.

'Not for another half-hour, Melanie,' her employer informed her. 'The food won't spoil, will it?'

'Not at all.' The smoked salmon entrée was already on its serving plates under cling-film and would keep indefinitely. The Thai pork main course was an easy stir-fry with all the ingredients pre-prepared, and the coconut caramel pudding was sitting in the refrigerator, only needing to be popped in the microwave for a couple of minutes.

Melanie had found through experience that dinner parties went more smoothly if as much of the menu as possible could be prepared or cooked beforehand. That way, delays posed no real problem. It also eliminated the possibility of last-minute cooking disasters.

Of course no amount of 'being prepared' could have prepared her for the perturbing influence of Mr Royce Grantham.

'Before I go, Byron,' she said, still marvelling at the coolness she was superficially exhibiting, 'I took the liberty of choosing the table wines for you. I hope you don't mind, but the whites did have to be chilled. The reds, of course, can easily be changed, if they don't meet with your approval.'

'Melanie, my dear, your ability to choose wines to complement your excellent cooking is only exceeded by your unflappability under fire. I was telling Royce earlier what a treasure you are. He seemed to think that my inviting him home to dinner at the last minute might cause a stir, but I assured him you were rarely rattled by anything.'

'And I told Byron,' Royce said from beside her shoulder, 'that if he didn't watch it, I might steal you away from him. I am in need of a housekeeper of your calibre for my home back in England.'

'My God, did you hear that, everyone?' Byron laughed. 'He's trying to seduce Melanie away from us. You've got Buckley's, Royce. Melanie's practically one of the family. Besides, she knows I'd be lost without her. Ava, my dear, your glass is nearly empty. Come over here and I'll top it up.'

'I'll double your salary,' Royce offered quietly before Melanie could escape his insidious presence.

She glanced up over her shoulder at him, only to have those wicked blue eyes clamp on to hers with a resolve that was frightening.

'I'll give you anything you want,' he stated boldly, 'if you come with me.'

'What I want, Mr Grantham,' she returned shakily, 'is for you to leave me alone.'

'Liar.'

Melanie turned fully to stare at him. 'How dare you?' she whispered fiercely under her breath.

'Are you Byron's mistress? Is that it?'

Now her eyes and nostrils flared wide, and a small smile pulled at his hard mouth. 'Don't bother to answer. I can see that you aren't. Just as well. I wouldn't have liked that. No, I wouldn't have liked that at all.'

His voice was low and hushed, so that the others could not overhear. But for all its softness, it was no less commanding, and quite terrifyingly hypnotic. 'Sorry to be this crass—it's not normally my style—but I have so little time. I've always found that if you want something badly enough, then sometimes the only way to get it is to go after it, boots and all. I want you, Melanie Lloyd. It's as simple as that. I find you breathtakingly beautiful and incredibly intriguing and so damned sexy I'll have to have ten cold showers when I get back to my hotel room tonight. Unless, of course, you're there with me...'

Melanie caught her breath. My God, did he honestly expect her to do such an outrageous thing? Had other silly females come running when he clicked his fingers at them?

Yes, she realised with a chilling acceptance of this man's success rate with women.

Fortunately, she had previous experience with a similar man which spelt out for her the danger inherent in surrendering one's will to an individual whose only concern was self.

Melanie summoned up what she considered her most withering look.

'I take it that's a no?' he drawled.

Without lowering herself even to give him an answer, she whirled away and strode rapidly from the drawing-room, hoping that her haste was construed by the others as need to hurry back to the kitchen and not the fleeing of a panic-stricken woman.

For underneath her very real fury at Royce for his arrogant presumption lay a startling susceptibility to his compliments.

It wasn't often that a woman was told she was breathtakingly beautiful and incredibly intriguing. Nor that she was so sexy that her pursuer would do anything to have her. Such talk could turn the head of any woman, let alone one as intrinsically lonely and possibly as frustrated as Melanie.

She had to constantly remind herself over the next half-hour of the type of man she was dealing with here. He was a daredevil who would employ any audacious tactics to get what he wanted. And that included flattery and outright lies. Next, he'd be telling her he *loved* her!

Still, it was damned hard not to imagine what spending the night in Royce Grantham's bed would be like.

It was all Joel's fault, she decided savagely as she raged around the kitchen. He had taught her how exciting sex could be with a man like him: how addictive even. She'd thought she'd been cured of such needs by his treachery, but it seemed she hadn't. Obviously, she was still a woman in its most basic sense, still a female animal, compelled by mother nature to mate with the male of her species.

I am not an animal, she argued as she set about removing the film on the entrées and arranging them on a tray. I am a human being. I do not have to give in to my baser instincts. I have will-power and pride to protect me from that marauding male in the drawing-room.

Ah, yes, pride. I've always been big on pride. Maybe too much so.

But not this time. This time pride will serve me well. Do I want to be reduced to nothing more than another sexual scalp on Royce Grantham's belt, another notch on his gun, another trophy for his memoirs?

'Over my dead body,' she muttered angrily.

Melanie glanced at the clock and felt her stomach tighten. Time to summon the guests to the dining-room and start serving the meal. Time to test her pride.

She did surprisingly well, she thought afterwards, though grateful that there was no soup on the menu. She probably would have slopped it everywhere, especially that first time their eyes met and he had the gall to smile at her.

Ten o'clock found her removing the plates from the main course and checking that everyone wanted dessert, and whether they wanted cream or not.

'Only a small helping for me, please, Melanie!' Ava said, smiling coyly. 'And no cream.'

'I thought you said you weren't dieting, Auntie,' Jade piped up.

Ava blushed. 'I'm not.'

'She certainly doesn't need to,' Royce put in suavely. 'I like a woman with a bit of meat on her.'

This comment was accompanied by a direct glance at Melanie's well-rounded bust. When an embarrassing heat zoomed into her cheeks she wanted to curl up and die. Gemma, for one, was looking at her curiously, as was Nathan. They know what's going on, she realised, and blushed all the more.

'Same here, Royce,' Byron was saying, totally ignorant of the by-play between his housekeeper and his guest. 'Once a woman reaches a certain age she looks better with her bones well covered.'

'I think that depends on the woman,' Jade said. 'Celeste Campbell must be pushing forty and she's reed-thin. I saw a photo of her in a women's magazine the other day, hosting some harbour party on her yacht. She was dressed in a bikini and looked sensational. I'd like to look half that good when I'm her age.'

'She probably does a lot of exercise,' Ava said with a sigh.

'Yes,' Byron snapped. 'All in her bedroom! For pity's sake, Jade, what is your fascination for that atrocious woman? You're always bringing her up.'

'Well, she is my aunt, you know,' Jade defended. 'Not to mention Whitmore Opals' main competition.'

'Maybe not for much longer.' Byron's smile was vengefully smug. 'I hear their sales are suffering since those reports appeared on television about their bribing Japanese tour companies to bypass all other duty-free stores in favour of theirs. I was wondering if you had something to do with those stories, Kyle. Not that I'm objecting, mind.'

'I may have dropped the right word in the right ear a while back,' he admitted coolly. 'I happen to own a part-share in the first television station to run that particular exposé.'

Byron laughed. 'I can see you're an invaluable man to have on our side. But surely, you're not going to continue being Whitmore's marketing manager indefinitely, are you?'

'No, I'm grooming Jade to take over next year. I really will have to get back to overseeing my own interests by then.'

'But surely Jade's too young and inexperienced!' her father argued. 'And she's going to have a baby. Her place is in the home, not in business!'

'Jade's place is where she's happiest,' Kyle defended firmly. 'Most women can combine a family and career these days if that's what they want. As for her being young and inexperienced ...she's actually better qualified than I am. Most of the new ideas Whitmore's have been successfully putting into practice over the past few weeks have been hers. I have great faith in her and I suggest you should too.'

'Enough of that, darling,' Jade intervened, laughing. 'I appreciate your support but I can fight my own battles. Pops, shut up and drink up. Melanie, I'll have a double helping of dessert, since I'm eating for two!'

Melanie suddenly realised she was still standing there, agonising over her earlier embarrassment, instead of getting dessert. She'd even forgotten who wanted cream and who didn't. All she could remember was that Ava only wanted a small helping. Flustered, she fled the room, deciding to put the cream in a jug so that people could serve themselves.

She waited as long as she could before putting the dessert plates on a tray and making her way back to the dining-room. The conversation around the table had moved on to the opal Royce supposedly wanted to buy, with both Jade and Kyle strongly vetoing any sale before the ball.

Melanie put the tray on the sideboard, placed the jug of cream in the centre of the table, then started placing a serving in front of each person, the smallest going to Ava, the largest to Jade.

'You'll have to stay on in Sydney for the auction if you want the Heart of Fire that badly,' Byron was saying to Royce as she gave her employer a slice of pudding. 'What's another fortnight to secure something so unique and precious? You won't get another opportunity, you know. Thanks, Melanie.'

Once again, Royce managed to catch her eye as he spoke. 'I couldn't agree more. Yes, I think I will stay till the ball, after which I'm going to take my unique and precious find straight back to England. I've a mind to see it adorn my home there. I have just the spot—in the master bedroom.'

Melanie reefed her eyes away. Was he really talking about the opal? Or herself? Despite all her earlier resolves, she found her mind filled with images of herself in that master bedroom. Herself and Royce.

Help me, pride, she prayed. Help me...

'But what if someone bids higher?' Gemma asked.

'I doubt they will. I've always been prepared to spend as much money as is necessary to get something I really want.'

Now Melanie's black eyes flashed his way again from where she was standing behind Byron's shoulder. So that was his strategy, was it? If all else fails, bring out the cheque-book. My God, did he honestly think he could *buy* her?

'You really want our pride and joy that much, eh?' Byron said.

'I certainly do.'

'Then we'll see you at the ball?'

'Most assuredly. I'll pop down to the shop and pick up tickets tomorrow morning. You'll be there, will you, Mrs Whitmore?' he directed at Gemma.

'Yes, of course,' she smiled, thinking to herself that he really was quite charming. And obviously very taken with Melanie. Why, he couldn't take his eyes off her every time she came into the room.

'No, I'm afraid you won't be, darling,' Nathan said, astonishing her. She sat there stunned for a second, while he spoke directly to Royce. 'Gemma and I will be spending the day with my daughter. My ex-wife has an—er—appointment she can't get out of.'

'But...but...' Gemma finally started stammering.

He took her hand and patted it. 'I forgot to tell you about it, darling. But not to worry. I'll telephone the store manager personally and smooth things over for you. They can call in one of the casuals. Really, there's no big problem, is there Byron?'

'Of course not. You're only working there as a little hobby, after all, Gemma.'

CHAPTER FOUR

GEMMA'S annoyance with Nathan was momentarily exceeded by outrage at Byron for speaking so patronisingly about her job.

Why, her sales figures were better than any of the other girls'! And she spoke Japanese much more fluently than anyone in the store, because she'd worked very hard at mastering the difficult language. Neither did she shy away from using it as some of the others did. In fact, she'd been so successful with Japanese tourists that they often asked especially for her.

'I don't think of my job as a hobby, Byron,' she said, trying not to sound as hurt as she felt.

'I should say not!' Jade jumped to her defence. 'What an old chauvinist you are, Pops. Take no notice of him, Gemma. I don't.'

'So I've noticed,' her father retorted drily. 'I'm glad Kyle's taken over your reins, daughter, dear. It'll be good to let someone else worry about you in the future.'

'Why should I worry about Jade?' Kyle shrugged. 'She's a grown woman with a mind of her own and more nous than most men I know. As for taking over her reins . . . my God, if I started telling Jade what to do or how to behave, she'd have me for breakfast.'

'You'd better believe it,' she said with a determined-sounding laugh. 'You're going to marry a liberated lady here and don't ever forget it!'

'Better you than me, Kyle,' her father pronounced. 'There again, to each his own. I have to admit that I prefer the old-fashioned kind of wife.'

'Amen to that,' Nathan muttered under his breath.

Gemma closed her eyes momentarily against the gatherings of a headache. Jade had just put her finger on the root cause of her unhappiness, and Nathan had just

49

verified it. He didn't want the sort of partnership Kyle and Jade had, where they shared everything on an equal footing—careers included. He wanted a wife of the old brigade, one who always deferred to her husband's opinion, one whose needs and ambitions were not considered or taken seriously, one whose only job was to keep her hubby happy—especially in the bedroom.

No doubt, at the appropriate time and when it suited him, Nathan would make her pregnant, after which she would be expected to give up her 'hobby' and retire to become an old-fashioned mother.

Gemma found it incredible that the thought of having Nathan's baby no longer gave her the pleasure it once would have. Dear heaven, hadn't she told Ma just before leaving Lightning Ridge that her dearest dream was to marry a nice man and have loads of babies? And hadn't she written to her old friend after marrying Nathan and told Ma she couldn't wait to have that big family she'd always wanted? Now here she was, shrinking from even having *one* baby.

But how could she look forward to pregnancy, if it meant she would have to leave a job she enjoyed, only to be imprisoned at home with no one to talk to and nothing to do? Nathan would probably also veto her doing any of the housework and cooking, just as he'd started vetoing other things he thought weren't good for her, such as seeing Royce again.

The bottom line was he was treating her like a child, making decisions for her, not trusting her judgement, acting like an autocratic father rather than the caring, loving husband she'd mistakenly thought he would be.

'Coffee, Gemma?'

Gemma opened her eyes and smiled a wan smile over her shoulder at Melanie. 'Yes, please.'

Melanie's returning smile as she placed the cup of coffee on the table had a sisterly understanding behind it that made Gemma feel better, and oddly stronger. In the absence of Ma, Gemma considered calling Melanie some time in the near future and asking her for advice on how best to tackle her problem. After all, she'd been married once. Maybe Melanie could advise if a new bride should fight openly for what she wanted right from the start, or try to achieve change in more subtle manipulative ways.

Take the problem she was faced with tomorrow. Gemma wanted to go to work. She suspected that Nathan's excuse about their having to take Kirsty was probably a lie. Even if it was true, she knew darned well that the last person Kirsty wanted to spend a day with was herself. The girl still hadn't really forgiven her for marrying her father, and thereby smashing her dream of her father getting back with her mother. Not once since their marriage had Kirsty visited them, or wanted Gemma with her father when he took her out. Even on her recent birthday, she'd bluntly told Nathan that Gemma wasn't welcome at her party.

Gemma believed if she didn't go to work tomorrow she would end up spending the day in the unit alone, just because Nathan had some weird idea in his brain that Royce Grantham was interested in her. What was wrong with her husband? Hadn't he seen for himself the various looks the Englishman had given Melanie all evening? He'd hardly given *her* a glance, or directed more than polite conversation her way.

Gemma suspected that this was one problem that couldn't be solved with subtle methods. She would have to stand up for her rights and make Nathan understand how she felt about his treating her like some silly girl with no mind of her own.

Yet the thought of an argument later that night was an upsetting and daunting one. Things had already been strained between them since their confrontation over Royce earlier in the day. Maybe she should just give in to Nathan's wishes this once. Gemma supposed it wasn't every day that a champion racing car driver would cross her path. It was probably his reputation with women that was bothering Nathan.

This thought started her thinking about what such a man would want from Melanie. Was he only looking for a holiday fling, some woman to show him a good time while he was here in Sydney? Or was the attraction deeper than that? Maybe he was on the lookout for a wife, now that he'd retired from his dangerous sport. Though, somehow, Gemma doubted it. Royce Grantham didn't look the marrying kind. Which only left an affair.

But Melanie was not the sort of woman to indulge in casual sex, of that Gemma felt certain. Frankly, in the months Gemma had known her, she'd shown no interest in men whatsoever. At first, Gemma had believed this had been due to her husband and baby being killed in that accident, but as she got to know her better Gemma wondered if her marriage had been a happy one. Sometimes, Melanie showed an icy contempt for the male sex that the tragedy alone could not explain.

Before tonight, Gemma would have thought any man's chances of attracting Melanie were less than zero, but there was no doubting Royce Grantham had made an impression on the normally indifferent housekeeper. A couple of times, Gemma had caught them exchanging highly charged looks, and once Melanie had actually blushed. This in itself was so unlike the other woman that Gemma had to revise her thinking on what Melanie might and might not do. Gemma herself knew how vulnerable a female could be when a man had set his sights on her seduction.

When she sighed, Nathan turned to her. 'You haven't drunk your coffee, darling. Is there anything wrong with it?'

'What? Oh...no...no, I was just daydreaming.'

'About what?'

'Nothing really. I'm tired, I guess.'

'Then perhaps we should go home. Byron, Gemma's a bit on the weary side. Would you mind if we left as soon as we've finished our coffee?'

'But it's only eleven,' he complained. 'And I was going to talk to you about the play.'

'There's no need. I've already made up my mind about that. I'll do it.'

'You *will*? Even with Lenore in the leading role?' Clearly, Byron was astonished. So was Gemma. She simply stared at her husband, totally speechless.

'I don't see why that should present a problem,' he drawled dismissively. 'Our divorce was quite amicable, no matter what others believe. To be honest, now that Lenore and I are no longer living together, we're better friends than ever.'

Gemma's whole insides contracted as a past incident suddenly jumped into her mind. It had happened the very first day Nathan had brought her here to Belleview to be his daughter's minder, at a time when she had already fallen under his spell, and when he'd subsequently claimed he was already smitten with her. Yet that night she'd stumbled across him kissing Lenore in the billiard-room, their embrace so passionate that neither of them had seen her standing in the doorway. She'd always meant to ask Nathan about that kiss, but had never seemed able to drum up the courage. Then, when he'd asked her to marry him, scorning any feelings for his ex-wife, she'd driven any worry about that kiss— or his still being in love with Lenore—to the back of her mind.

Now the worries resurfaced. She didn't want him directing Lenore in that play, didn't want him spending that much time with her. The woman was exquisitely beautiful, her elegance and sophistication always making Gemma feel a little gauche by comparison. No doubt she knew exactly how to please the man sexually, whereas Gemma still had moments of shyness and inhibition in that department.

Gemma's stomach churned when she thought of Lenore happily having pleasured Nathan in all sorts of erotic ways during their marriage. Feelings of inadequacy and jealousy burnt within her, and she resolved that she would be more daring in the bedroom in future, and not pull back from some of Nathan's more adventurous suggestions like some prudish virgin. Usually he laughed gently at her embarrassed reactions, then simply moved on to some other more acceptable activity or po-

sition. But how soon before his outer patience waned
and he began to find her boring?

With these new concerns revolving round in her mind,
Gemma decided not to make an issue of going to work
tomorrow. Best take the line of least resistance this time.
She didn't want Nathan angry with her when he started
directing Lenore in that play...

But all her good intentions went out the window when,
a few minutes into their silent drive home, Nathan said
crossly, 'I don't like it when you sulk.'

Indignation and a sudden flaring of temper sent her
eyes snapping his way. 'I'm not sulking. But even if I
were, then you shouldn't be too surprised. I would just
be acting the way you've been treating me all night. Like
a child!'

'Don't be ridiculous, Gemma. I've done no such
thing.'

'What do you call it then when you tell me I'm not
going to work tomorrow, simply because you think Royce
Grantham might make a line for me? Blind Freddie could
see that the woman Royce has set his sights on is Melanie,
not me. Good grief, Nathan, didn't you see the way he
looked at her tonight?'

'I saw. But I know Melanie. She won't come across,
which means Mr Grantham will be left with a severe
case of frustration which he will seek to ease with the
next available female. Namely you!'

Gemma threw her hands in the air. 'I don't believe
this. Anyone would think I didn't have any say in who
I chose to go to bed with. Why would I want Royce
Grantham when it's *you* I want, *you* I love? Or don't
you believe I truly love you, Nathan?'

There was an electric silence till they pulled up at a
red light, where Nathan slowly turned his head her way.
His face was irritatingly unreadable, those grey eyes of
his both cool and steady. 'All I'm trying to do is protect
my wife from the sort of man most women have few
defences against, let alone a young inexperienced girl
like you. This is not a question of love, Gemma, but a

question of lust. Believe it or not, a woman can love one man and still be made to feel lust for another.'

'I don't believe that.'

'Of course you don't, but there again, you're only twenty years old. Your opinion might change in a few years. To give you an example, however, my erstwhile ex-wife loved another man during our entire marriage. But she thoroughly enjoyed going to bed with me, I can assure you.'

Gemma gasped in shock. 'I don't believe you.'

His mouth twisted into a sardonic smile. 'Which part don't you believe?'

Gemma's thoughts whirled. She could hardly refute that Nathan enjoyed making love to her. She'd seen the evidence before her own eyes. As for Lenore's being in love with someone else... If Nathan said that was so she supposed it was. It would certainly explain the divorce, and his bitterness. Despite what he'd said to-night at dinner, he hadn't been happy about the divorce. Was that because he *was* still in love with Lenore? Maybe, when he spoke of being able to love one person and lust after another, he was talking about himself.

A grim bleakness swept into Gemma's heart. Maybe Nathan had married her simply because he lusted after her. Maybe he'd never loved her. Now that she thought about it, he'd never actually said he did. He'd said he wanted her and adored her but he never used the word 'love'.

'Do you love me, Nathan?' she asked shakily.

Now, his steely composure broke. 'What kind of stupid question is that? Of course I do. Good God, why do you think I married you?'

'I'm not sure,' she said, bewildered and unhappy. 'Why don't you tell me.'

'I married you because I love you, dammit! Surely you're not going to be one of those women who want to be told that every day, are you?'

Gemma shook her head. Why did admitting that he loved her make him angry? Or was it her forcing him to *talk* that made him angry?

'No,' she sighed, still not at all sure that he did. It brought her mind back to the woman at the core of her doubts. 'Who is Lenore in love with?'

'I'm not at liberty to say.'

'Why not?'

'The man's married and still living with his wife and family.'

Gemma gasped. 'And Lenore's sleeping with him?'

'You don't think she's living the life of a nun, do you? Who do you think she's spending tomorrow with?'

'My God...'

'Does that shock you?' His laughter was harsh and dry. 'Good. Maybe now your rose-coloured glasses about people might begin to smear a little.'

Gemma fell silent, her mind fighting to separate reality from Nathan's cruel cynicism. He wasn't above trying to paint Lenore as morally and sexually loose, simply to persuade her to his point of view that most people were like that—or *could* be like that, given the right circumstances.

Gemma's natural aversion to such cynicism had her trying to put aside her natural jealousy of Lenore and see her as she really was. Past memories provided a picture, not of a Jezebel, but a strong-minded woman of good character and strength. Lenore was a decent woman, Gemma decided, not a scarlet one.

'Are you suggesting Lenore slept with this man while she was married to you?' she asked, disbelief in her voice.

'How should I know? Maybe she did and maybe she didn't. She *says* she didn't. But as I've already said, Lenore wasn't unhappy in my bed, which proves my point that love and lust can coexist in the same person.'

'Maybe with Lenore but not with me,' she stated firmly. 'And not with a lot of other people, I'll warrant.'

'You say that because you're young and inexperienced.'

'I thought you *liked* the fact that I was young and inexperienced,' she argued, her frustration acute.

'I do,' he insisted.

'Maybe you'd rather I was more like Lenore?' she flung at him, stung by a mental picture of Lenore doing those things she still felt inhibited about.

'Good God, no! Why ever would you say such a thing?'

'Perhaps because I saw you kissing Lenore one night and *both* of you were certainly enjoying it, not just your ex-wife!'

Thank God they were stationary, the way Nathan's head whipped round. 'What in God's name are you talking about?'

She told him, watching as his frown smoothed into a sardonic smile. 'Oh, yes, I remember.' He laughed then. 'I suppose you won't believe me when I say that wasn't Lenore I was kissing that night. It was a certain young woman in a sexy pink sundress who'd aroused me to a fever pitch of desire. Lenore said something that touched a nerve and before I knew it I was taking my frustration out on her. Being the mature, sensible woman that she is, she went along with it for a diplomatic minute or two before kicking me delicately in the shins and thereby bringing me to my senses.'

His self-mocking tone did not entirely soothe Gemma's doubts. 'So you're not still in love with her?'

'Heaven forbid! But your wording suggests I once was. I never loved Lenore, nor she me. She flirted with me one night in an attempt to get back at her beloved who would have none of her, and I took her up on the unspoken invitation. We went to bed and she got pregnant with Kirsty. She refused to have an abortion and I refused to spawn a bastard, so we got married and tried to make the best of it.'

The light turned green and the Mercedes purred forwards. Nathan's smile was relaxed now as he looked over at her. 'Have you been harbouring these silly doubts all the time?'

She nodded, indeed feeling silly. But none of this entirely eliminated the fact that Nathan clearly had no faith or trust in a woman's love, hers included. No doubt Lenore's behaviour was responsible for this. It seemed incredible to Gemma that a woman could love one man and enjoy sleeping with another. Though she had to concede that if that man was Nathan there were extenuating circumstances. Not only was he incredibly handsome with a beautiful body, but he was a superb lover, very knowledgeable about a woman's body and how to give it pleasure. He seemed genuinely to adore female flesh. The feel of it, and the taste. He did things to her with his hands and mouth that made her quiver all over just thinking about them.

She jumped when his hand came over and covered her knee.

'Wait till I get you home and I'll show you just how much I love you,' he rasped.

Gemma tried not to tense. Was this his only way of showing her he loved her?

For the rest of the drive home, Gemma couldn't help mulling over what he'd said about lust and love. Could people always differentiate between the two? Might someone think they were genuinely in love when in fact they were in the grip of lust? If so, what happened when their lust began to wane, when suddenly there was nothing left to base a relationship—or marriage—on?

Gemma arrived back at their unit, tense and afraid. The last thing she wanted now was for her husband to make love to her.

CHAPTER FIVE

MELANIE was stacking the dishwasher when Royce walked into the kitchen, a brandy balloon in one hand and a cigar in the other. Melanie didn't say a word, eyeing him coldly as he walked over and slid up on to one of the breakfast bar stools. He eyed her back with an insouciant smile, giving the amber liquid a couple of swirls before lifting it to his lips.

'Good cognac, this,' he said, putting the drink down to take a deep drag on the cigar.

'I don't allow smoking in my kitchen,' she said frostily, and slid a small souvenir ashtray on to the counter in front of him.

'No trouble.' Stubbing the end of the cigar into the picture of the Opera House, he left its smouldering remains there and returned to a leisurely sipping of the cognac.

Melanie folded her arms and glared at him. 'If you're going to offer me a job as your housekeeper again then forget it. There isn't enough money in the world to induce me to work for you.'

'Not to worry. I've given up on that idea.'

'But you haven't given up on *me*, have you? If you had, you wouldn't be here now.' Her hands unfolded to rest on her hips, her aggressive stance allowing her simmering fury better expression. 'What excuse did you give Byron for a trip to the kitchen? Or is this a detour from the powder-room?'

'Carrying cognac and a cigar? Hardly. No, I told him the truth.'

'You told him you wanted to chat up the cook?'

'*Chat up* the cook?' His expression was one of mock innocence. 'Now why would I want to chat up a woman who's made it perfectly clear she's not interested in me?

Or am I mistaken...?' His eyes narrowed upon her face and its undeniably high colour. 'Perhaps you always play this game with men who are as passionately attracted to you as I am. Perhaps it adds something to your eventual capitulation to give them a hard time first.'

'You're mad!' she gasped.

'Yes,' he agreed smoothly. 'About you. And I don't think you're as indifferent as you pretend to be. Your body language is a dead giveaway, Melanie, as is the intensity of your so-called outrage. I think you just might want me as much as I want you.'

Melanie achieved composure with a supreme effort of will. Her gaping mouth snapped shut, her lips pursing in a parody of primness. She consoled herself with the fact that Royce couldn't possibly see into her mind, into the awful fantasy that was video-playing there in full CinemaScope.

'What a ghastly man you are!' she snapped, angrier with herself than with him. 'And you couldn't be more wrong. I detest men like you. *Detest* them, I tell you!'

'"The lady doth protest too much methinks,"' he drawled, and drained the brandy.

Much to Melanie's consternation, he put down the now empty balloon, slid off the stool and began making his way around to where she was virtually imprisoned in the galley-style kitchen, her only escape quickly blocked by Royce's approaching body.

She shrank back into the far corner, eyes wide, heart beating wildly in her chest. 'If you touch me, I'll scream!'

He stopped an arm's length away from her, his almost handsome face tipping to one side as he surveyed her own stricken features with curiosity and dark puzzlement. 'I think, perhaps, you mean it.'

'I *do*!'

For several tormenting seconds he just stood there, watching her, narrowed eyes raking over the rise and fall of her breasts before lifting once again to her flushed face.

'No,' he denied at last with a confidence that totally threw her. 'You don't.'

If he'd grabbed her roughly, she might still have screamed. But he didn't. He drew her trembling body to his quite slowly, tipping her chin up even more slowly, holding her wide black eyes with his hard blue eyes for ages before his mouth descended.

Melanie hated herself for standing there and allowing him to kiss her. She especially hated that it was *her* lips which parted first. Immediately, Royce deepened the kiss, shattering any illusion Melanie might have been holding that she could resist this man. Her bones went to water beneath the onslaught of his mouth and tongue and soon she was clinging to him, clinging and moaning softly.

'Oh, God, Melanie,' Royce groaned, breaking the kiss to press impassioned lips to her throat. 'Come back to the hotel with me tonight. I've already asked Byron if you could have tomorrow off. I said I was going to ask you to show me around Sydney but he seemed to think you wouldn't agree.' His mouth covered her ear, making her shiver uncontrollably when his tonguetip traced the shell-like opening then dipped inside. 'He doesn't know the real you, does he?'

The real you...

Royce's words cut through the haze of her arousal like a knife, stabbing deep into her heart.

The real you...

She wrenched back out of his arms and might have slapped him across the face if she'd been quicker. But he easily grabbed her wrists, holding them in front of her heaving chest while he shook his head in wry reproach. 'Don't, Melanie. It's not necessary. I *like* the real you.'

'You don't know what you're talking about,' she cried, humiliation sparking a defiant anger. 'You don't know the real me. You'll never know the real me!'

'Then I'll settle for the Melanie I just kissed, and who kissed me back with such passion. That's the Melanie I want to know.'

'Oh, I don't doubt it,' she scorned, yanking her hands out of his grasp. 'The trouble is, I don't want you to know *any* Melanie. I don't like you, Royce Grantham.'

His laughter was dry. 'Then you have a funny way of showing it.'

'Has it occurred to you that you might have struck me at a weak moment?' she flung at him, determined to dent his ego a little while finding an escape for herself. 'Maybe I'm simply in need of a man. *Any* man. You know what widows are like,' she jeered. 'They can get quite desperate.'

'And is that what you are, Melanie?' he taunted softly. 'Desperate?'

'Not so desperate that I would go to bed with the likes of you!'

His eyes darkened, his face hardening. 'I'm getting tired of this game, Melanie. You're going to spend the weekend with me and that's that!'

'I most certainly am not!'

She could see the muscles clenched hard in his jaw. 'Don't be so bloody stupid.'

'And don't you be so bloody arrogant!'

'Melanie, for pity's sake...'

She laughed a hard, bitter sound. 'Don't you talk to me of pity, Royce Grantham. That word isn't in your vocabulary. Now go away. I have no intention of going back to your hotel with you tonight or of showing you around Sydney this weekend.'

He slanted her a long, thoughtful look. 'Is that your final word on the matter?'

'It is.'

'I could kiss you again, you know, and show you up for the hypocrite you are.'

Fear zoomed into her eyes, bringing irritation and confusion to Royce's face.

'I don't understand you, Melanie Lloyd. If you weren't attracted to me, I could accept being rejected. If you were involved with another man, I might even back off in gracious defeat. But there is no other man, is there? I wonder what it is that frightens you so much about me...'

'You don't frighten me,' she defended, but lamely.

'Oh, yes, I do. I terrify the life out of you. And I aim to find out why. I'll accept your right to say no tonight, but this isn't the end of us. Not by a long shot. I'll be calling you tomorrow, and the next day, and the next. And sooner or later you'll either tell me the truth or you'll give in and go out with me.'

Whirling on his heels, he strode back around the long counter and stalked from the room. Melanie was left to stare blankly after him, her panic receding once he disappeared from view, quickly replaced by outrage. The hide of the man, the utter gall! He needed to be taught lessons in humility *and* rejection. And by God, she was going to teach them to him.

Oh, really? came a darkly mocking voice from deep inside. Easy to say but not so easy to do. What happens if he kisses you again? Can you honestly say that he couldn't make you want him as you were wanting him a little while ago? What if he'd pushed that encounter a little further, touched your breasts for instance?

Melanie shuddered as just thinking about Royce touching her like that had her nipples hardening inside her bra. God, but he probably could have had her here tonight, in the kitchen, if he'd been daring enough.

She groaned her dismay. Had he known that? Had he sensed her vulnerability to daring men? Was that why he'd kissed her even after she'd warned him not to?

She sincerely hoped not. What hope did she have of warding him off if he realised her response to that kiss had resulted from his being bold, if he knew she found his ruthless resolve to pursue her both exciting and arousing? Her only salvation was making him believe she'd been simply suffering from a momentary frustration tonight. She *was* a widow, after all. A widow who didn't date. Ever.

The noise of footsteps had Melanie's eyes jerking round in the direction of the open doorway. But it was only Byron, undoing his cufflinks as he walked in.

'Well, that's it,' he pronounced. 'Everyone's gone home. Kyle offered Royce a lift back to town and he went. I dare say I have you to thank for his early exit.'

'Me?'

Byron chuckled. 'He seemed most put out after his little visit to the kitchen. I did warn Royce that you wouldn't go out with him, but he simply wouldn't listen. Our Melanie never goes out with men, I said. You're wasting your time.'

Melanie stiffened. For some reason, Byron's amusement rankled. 'How do you know that?' she challenged.

Byron looked up from his cufflinks. 'Know what?'

'That I don't go out with men.'

Byron looked startled before a frown settled on his handsome features. 'What are you trying to tell me, Melanie? That you *do*? I'm afraid I don't believe that. You've made your feelings quite clear about men, my dear. And I understand. Truly.'

You understand *nothing*, Byron, she thought bitterly. You *know* nothing.

'Did Royce do or say something to upset you?' Byron asked abruptly.

'No, of course not,' she sighed.

His glance was thoughtful. 'Maybe you should have gone out with him. Maybe it's time...'

Her chin shot up. 'Time for what, Byron?'

'Time you started living again,' he said. 'You've changed lately, my dear. Haven't you noticed? You're taking more of an interest in things around you instead of just going about your work like some robot. When I told Royce you'd become like one of the family, then you have, of late.'

Melanie was taken aback by Byron's observations till she realised it was true. The change had probably started with Nathan bringing both Kirsty and Gemma home to Belleview to live some weeks back. It had been impossible to maintain a remote distance from two such engaging young people. Suddenly, the household had been full of laughter and fun. Melanie's coldly bitter heart had started to thaw, there was no doubt about that. She'd begun to care about people again. Why, when Nathan and Gemma had eloped, she'd really worried about the girl. That was why she'd gone to town today to visit Gemma and to reassure herself that the girl was happy.

She frowned when the thought came that Gemma hadn't seemed too happy tonight at dinner...

Melanie jumped when Byron suddenly touched her on the shoulder. 'Go to bed, my dear. You look tired. Don't worry about breakfast for me in the morning. I'll be up early going to golf. I'll get myself something at the club-house. Thanks again for that splendid meal tonight. You do spoil us, you know. Lord knows what we'll do if you ever decide to leave us.' With a warm smile, he turned and left the room.

Melanie sighed and turned away to finish clearing up the kitchen. Yes, she mused as she worked, she had changed. Her emotions, once dead, had stirred to life. Byron was right. Time to live again. In a fashion...

She would never be the same person she'd been before Joel. That was impossible. The one emotion she could never recapture was the ability to love and trust a man. Which meant marriage was out. As for having another baby... She could never face motherhood again, either. Even looking at a baby sometimes brought so much pain that she avoided women with prams.

So, if she was going to live again, what was she going to do differently in future?

Melanie hated the way her mind automatically flew to Royce Grantham. But it very definitely did. And it stayed on him. Stayed and stayed and stayed.

'Damn the man!' she muttered, and, with the last dirty plate cleared away, she marched down to her bedroom which was opposite the laundry.

She undressed quickly and angrily, throwing her skirt and blouse across her chair and stuffing her stockings and underwear into the small cane linen basket in the corner. But as she went to snatch a nightie out from under the pillow she caught a glimpse of her naked body in the cheval-glass in the corner. Her breath caught, her heart thudding as she stared at herself.

As though compelled, she turned and walked over to survey her nude body, her hands lifting to cover herself in an oddly defensive gesture, as though by doing so she wouldn't see the evidence of her own arousal. Slowly, shakily, her hands slid down from her hard-tipped breasts to her tensely held stomach, and finally, finally, she accepted the strong possibility of her having an affair with Royce. He'd been so right. She wanted him probably more than he wanted her, wanted him so much it was an ache deep inside her body.

A shudder ripped through her with this acceptance, a wave of heat following in its path. Reaching up, she took the pins from her hair and let it tumble in blue-black waves around her shoulders. She imagined what it would feel like to stand like this in front of Royce, to watch those sexy blue eyes of his take her in, watch them glitter with desire.

The intensity of her response to such thinking shook her. God, but she had no hope of resisting him, no hope at all!

And why *should* she resist him? suggested a wicked voice she didn't recognise as her own. Why shouldn't you have what men like Royce have been having for years? An exciting sex life without any strings attached, without consequences, without commitment? Let's face it, there's no chance of you falling in love with a man like him. You've been down that path before and have no intention of going down it again. All you have to do is protect yourself...

Melanie stared at herself in the mirror, appalled yet intrigued. Being appalled won in the end and she spun away, dragging out her nightie and pulling it down over her head. She dived into bed and buried her face in the pillow, doing a good imitation of pretending to go to sleep.

But that insidious idea wouldn't let go. It kept coming back, as ruthless as the man who'd inspired it. Desire invaded her mind, but so did a strange strength of will, a new sense of herself as a living breathing female. Apparently, the shell she'd cocooned her sexuality within for years had been smashed with a vengeance today, and a new woman was emerging, a tougher, harder, but highly sensual creature who would have what she wanted without putting herself at risk of the sort of pain she'd endured in the past. It was love that brought pain, she decided, not passion. She would have one without succumbing to the other. She would have Royce, but on *her* terms, not his.

Coming to such a scandalous decision rocked Melanie. Was this the woman who had allowed Joel to control every aspect of their life together, who had always had difficulty making decisions of any magnitude? The one time she *had* made a big decision had resulted in tragedy. Maybe this would have a similar outcome...

Don't be ridiculous, the new Melanie argued. Would you rather become a wimpy victim, waiting anxiously for Royce to call, worrying over when he was going to seduce you, seemingly against your will? Where's the pride in that, let alone the self-respect? You're a grown woman, with normal healthy needs and desires. Who better to satisfy those needs and desires temporarily but a man like Royce who is just passing through?

Do it, that wicked voice tempted. But do it your way!

Before she could think better of it, Melanie jumped out of bed and hurried out into the corridor and along to the kitchen where she wrenched open the cupboard that housed the telephone directories. On finding the number of the Regency Hotel, she jotted it down on the notepad she kept near the phone, ripped off the page, shoved the directory back, slammed the cupboard door and returned to her room with its own private line.

Her hands were shaking as she dialled but she was determined not to back out. The receptionist at the hotel put her straight through to Royce's room, despite the hour—it was after one. Her nerve only began to fail when no one answered for ages. At last, the receiver was disconnected and Royce snapped hello.

'Royce?' she said, nerves making her voice curt.

'Yes,' he grunted. 'Who is this?'

'It's Melanie.'

The line fell silent.

Melanie gulped, then plunged on. 'I've decided to make a counter-suggestion for tomorrow, if you're still interested.'

Again, all she got was dead silence.

'Well, are you?' she snapped

'I'm getting over my shock, if you don't mind.'

Her laugh was harsh. 'What shock? You were pretty confident of success with me, weren't you? I've decided to simply pre-empt your next move and go straight to the heart of the matter.'

'Which is?'

'Our going to bed together.'

She had to smile over his sharply indrawn breath.

'What's the problem, Royce? Did I read you wrong? Are you saying all you wanted me for was as a tour guide after all?'

'For God's sake, Melanie, stop talking like this. It isn't you at all!'

Again she laughed. 'As I told you before, Royce, you don't know the real me.'

'Are you saying this is the real you?'

'Could be. It's certainly the only one you're going to get. Take it or leave it.'

He startled her with another elongated silence.

'I'll take it,' he said at last, his words brusque.

'I thought you might. Do you have a pen and paper handy?'

'I think so...' She heard the sound of a drawer opening and shutting. 'What am I supposed to be writing down?'

'An address where you can pick me up tomorrow night.'

'Why not at Belleview?'

'Oh, no, I can't have that. What would Byron think?'

'Who gives a stuff what Byron thinks?'   –

'I do. Can you get a car? I have an aversion to taxis, especially on Saturday night. They drive like lunatics.'

'I can hire one, I suppose.'

'Good. Here's the address...' He repeated it back to her after he'd written it down. 'If you get a map you should be able to find it easily enough. After all, you've got all day.'

'What time do you want me to pick you up?'

'Eight. On the dot. Oh, and Royce...'

'Yes?'

'Don't come in. Blow the horn and I'll come out.'

She hung up, her heart pounding in her chest, her face flushed and her hands shaking. Yet when she'd spoken, she'd sounded so cool, so controlled. Had she developed a split personality? Was that it? The old Melanie and the new. If so, it was the old Melanie that resurfaced once she realised what she had done.

Oh, God, she groaned inwardly. God...

Her head dropped into her hands but there was no going back, no changing her mind. The new Melanie would not have allowed that. She'd set both Melanies on a course that had no turning. It went straight to hell!

CHAPTER SIX

'GEMMA!' Melanie exclaimed on opening the front door shortly before eleven on the Saturday morning. 'What are you doing here?'

'I came to see you.'

'*Me*?'

'Yes. Can we go somewhere private to talk? Who's home? Ava, I suppose. What about Byron?'

'Byron's at golf and Ava, surprisingly, has gone out. I think she's shopping and having her hair done.'

'So we're alone?'

'Yes, if you don't count the gardener out the back.'

Gemma sighed and stepped inside. 'That's a relief. I won't have to smile sweetly and pretend everything's fine.'

Gemma avoided Melanie's sharp look, turning away to take off her brown suede jacket and hang it up in the coat closet. One part of her wished she hadn't come—it was hard to admit to anyone at Belleview that her marriage to Nathan was already in trouble—but common sense told her she needed advice, preferably from an intelligent, level-headed woman of experience. Who better than Melanie?

Turning back, Melanie was still looking at her with a concerned expression on her face.

'You haven't left Nathan, have you?'

Gemma closed her eyes for a second. How odd that Melanie's question didn't produce the shock that it would have a few weeks back. When Nathan had assumed, after their little spat on their honeymoon, that she was leaving him, she'd been appalled. For *her* marriage was for life, not till divorce us do part. Now, she had to admit that leaving Nathan had crossed her mind. Especially this morning...

'Gemma?' Melanie repeated, sounding really worried now.

Sighing, she opened her eyes. 'No. I haven't left Nathan. Not yet, anyway.'

'That sounds ominous. Look, let's go sit together somewhere and you can tell me what's troubling you. Where shall we go?'

'How about the family-room? I always liked that room when I stayed here. It's not quite as intimidating as the rest of the house. No antiques or treasures to worry about knocking into.'

Melanie smiled a typical Melanie smile, Gemma thought. Very dry. She looked extra drab today too, her face devoid of all colour, her hair even more savagely scraped back than ever.

As she followed Melanie into the family-room, Gemma conceded that Royce Grantham wasn't going to succeed with her. Nathan had been right about that. Pity. It might have solved one of her own problems.

Sighing heavily, Gemma settled into one of the squashy brown leather armchairs facing the huge television set, a long low coffee-table in front of her.

'Shall I get coffee?' Melanie offered. 'I was just about to have a cup myself.'

'That would be nice. Thanks.'

'I'll also bring some of Ava's store of chocolate biscuits. She says she's not going to eat any more and you look as if you could do with some energy food.'

'I didn't sleep much last night.'

Gemma was taken aback by the odd expression that flashed across Melanie's normally expressionless black eyes. It was almost as if the other woman had been *amused* by something she'd said. Did she perhaps think Nathan had kept her awake all night making wonderfully satisfying love to her?

Gemma groaned silently. Maybe if that had been the case, she wouldn't be sitting here this morning. Oh, he'd wanted to make love, as usual, but the tension of the evening had taken its toll and for the first time she hadn't been able to respond to Nathan's kisses and caresses.

Nathan had become quite frustrated by her lack of response. His lovemaking had finally turned rough, as though he thought he could make her feel something if he kissed her more savagely, touched her more forcefully.

But his semi-violent attentions set off memories from the past that Gemma thought she'd forgotten. Suddenly, Nathan's mouth had become *his* mouth, Nathan's hands, *his* hands. She'd frozen beneath him, as she had once frozen beneath that vile brute. But where *he'd* been unable to do more than touch, Nathan was not similarly impotent.

When her husband drove his impassioned body deep inside Gemma, and set up a relentless rhythm, she was shocked out of her catatonic state. Guilt consumed her as she realised this was the man she loved, not some pig assaulting her. Just to lie there under him, frozen and unresponsive, was a dreadful thing to do.

So Gemma set about doing the one thing she thought she'd never have to do. Fake her pleasure. And she'd done it very well, so well that Nathan had groaned in triumph, his own climax seemingly more intense than ever before.

'You're still mine,' he'd muttered into her hair, possessive hands keeping her joined to him for a long, long time. When finally he'd fallen asleep, she'd eased her aching body away from under his and lain there, staring at the ceiling for hours. She'd felt empty and cold and unbearably depressed. She hadn't succumbed to sleep till shortly before dawn.

Nathan had woken her around nine with a breakfast tray and a message that he'd already rung her work to say she wouldn't be in. He'd kissed her, then stunned her by ordering her to stay home and not to answer the telephone or the door. When she'd gone to argue, he'd cut her dead, saying if she loved him she would do this for him. He would have taken her with him, he'd said but Kirsty still didn't want her to come. Interpreting her angry silence as co-operation, he'd congratulated her on showing good sense at last, reassured her he would be back in plenty of time to take her out tonight, kissed her again, then left.

For at least half an hour she'd lain there, not knowing what to do or where to turn, till she'd thought of Melanie. Immediately, she'd thrown back the duvet and leapt out of bed, showered and dressed, then driven out to Belleview. Now, here she was, sitting in the family-room, waiting for Melanie to return, feeling very uptight.

Leaning back in the softly padded chair, she took several steadying breaths, managing to feel a bit more relaxed by the time Melanie returned with the coffee and biscuits on a tray.

'I have to admit you've surprised me coming here this way,' Melanie said as she poured the coffee. 'When I dropped in to see you at work yesterday, you seemed so happy. What happened after I left you to change the *status quo*?'

Gemma shook her head. 'Well you might ask.'

'I *am* asking,' Melanie said, and handed her a cup of coffee.

'Royce Grantham happened, that's what,' Gemma said ruefully, and started sipping the coffee.

After a few silent seconds, she looked over to see Melanie was staring at her with a startled look on her face.

'Don't get the wrong idea,' Gemma rushed on. 'He didn't make a line for me or anything. I'm not blind, Melanie. I saw last night he was very taken with you. You're the reason he came into the shop in the first place. He...he must have seen you and fancied you. He came in and asked about you, said he thought he knew you.'

'That old chestnut.' A sardonic smile pulled at her mouth. 'One would have thought he'd have had more imagination. Still, it worked, I suppose. He found out where I was.'

Gemma couldn't quite make out Melanie's attitude. Was she glad Royce was interested enough in her to pursue her? Or angry? She sounded half amused, half bitter.

'What exactly did you tell him about me?' Melanie asked.

'Nothing much, really. Just that you worked for Byron. He started talking about the opal in the window after that. You know...the Heart of Fire. And then Nathan walked in and all hell broke loose.'

Melanie was taken aback. 'In what way?'

'Nathan recognised him. Naturally, I hadn't. I don't have a wide knowledge of world celebrities, especially sportsmen. Frankly, I'd never heard of Royce Grantham, let alone recognised him.'

'That's nothing to be ashamed of. Neither had I.'

'Yes, but I never recognise *anyone*. Anyway, Nathan assumed he was trying to chat me up. He refused to believe me when I said he was interested in you. He went on and on about him being a dangerous man when it came to women and said he was sure to show up to pester me again. I told him he was crazy and we...well...we had a bit of an argument about it. You can imagine what he thought when we arrived last night and "guess who" was already here. I nearly died.'

'You weren't the only one who was surprised,' Melanie admitted with understated sarcasm.

Gemma frowned. 'Don't you like him, Melanie? I thought...'

'He's a rogue and a scoundrel,' she snapped. 'I wouldn't trust him as far as I could throw him.'

Gemma's heart sank. 'That's what Nathan said. I...I thought he was rather nice.'

'*Nice*? He's a snake!'

'I suppose you think I'm naïve too.'

'I think you're very young.'

'Young and stupid,' Gemma muttered, miserable now. She'd thought Melanie would be on her side. Clearly, she'd been wrong.

'I didn't say that, Gemma. You're far from stupid.'

'Well, Nathan thinks I'm stupid. He treats me like a child most of the time. He wouldn't let me go to work today simply because he thought Royce might drop in.

He also ordered me not to answer the telephone or the door.'

'Oh, dear... He's trying to protect you, I suppose. Men like Royce Grantham can be very persistent, not to mention unscrupulous. Your being married wouldn't deter him, Gemma. Not even remotely. Still, I don't think you're in any immediate danger.'

'I wish you'd convince Nathan of that. The man's paranoid! Doesn't he realise that Tom Cruise could walk into my life and I wouldn't look at him twice? I love my husband, Melanie. Why doesn't he trust that love?'

'I don't know, Gemma. Nathan's a complex man. None of us knows him very well. I think things happened in his childhood and adolescence that affected him very deeply. Maybe if you asked him about his mother, and his upbringing...'

Gemma's laugh was caustic. 'I've tried that, believe me. He won't talk about the past, not even *mine*! Soon after we met, he told me he wanted to know all about my life up till now, but every time I start telling him about Lightning Ridge and my life with my father he finds some way of changing the subject.'

'To what? How?'

Gemma blushed. 'Mostly he starts making love to me. I...I like making love, but not as a substitute for every other kind of intimacy. I was watching Kyle and Jade with each other last night. Their camaraderie. Their sense of sharing. Their friendship. I felt so jealous. That's what *I* want, Melanie. That's what I *need*. I can't spend my whole life being nothing but a...a...'

'Possession?'

Gemma blinked.

'Well, that's all you feel like, isn't it?' Melanie went on with brutal frankness. 'Nathan's pretty little possession. His private toy. His very own creation.'

Gemma's eyes rounded. 'Yes! Yes, that's exactly what I feel like.'

'God help me for suggesting this,' Melanie muttered, 'but would a baby help, do you think?'

Gemma shook her head. 'Nathan says it's too soon.'

'What do *you* say?'

'I...I think it's too soon too.'

Melanie was clearly taken aback. 'You've surprised me. I would have thought motherhood was very important to you.'

'It is. It's just that...I'm not sure...'

'Of what?'

Gemma looked at Melanie, her eyes pained. 'I'm not sure Nathan really loves me.'

Melanie nodded, slowly, ruefully. 'I see.'

'I think he *thinks* he loves me,' she rushed on.

'But you think it's just lust.'

'I'm not sure...'

A silence fell between them for a short while.

'And what about you, Gemma? Are you sure what it is *you* feel for Nathan?'

Gemma's big brown eyes rounded. 'What...what do you mean? I love him.'

'Do you really? As I said, you're very young and he's a very handsome, virile man. Women can feel lust too, you know. Sometimes with dire results. Sometimes it propels them to marry men they should never have married. It blinds them to reality. And sometimes, sometimes it makes them do really dangerous things...'

Her voice had lowered to a husky whisper, her eyes glazing with a faraway, almost haunted look. But then suddenly, she snapped out of it, and that cold mask was solidly back in place.

'Only time will tell, I suppose,' she said firmly. 'Lust, you see, has a tendency to run its course. One day, if your feelings are only sexual, then the scales will fall from your eyes and you'll see the real man, not the mirage, and vice versa. So I think you're very wise not to have a baby, Gemma, till you are sure, both about *your* feelings, *and* Nathan's. Meanwhile, you must not let Nathan treat you in any manner which doesn't feel right to you, and that includes sexually. He has no *right* to your body, Gemma, just because he married you. If you don't want to make love, then say so.'

Gemma flushed, thinking about the night before. 'But what about . . . when *he* wants to, and you . . . well . . . you don't really mind but you can't seem to . . . enjoy it?'

'That's a difficult one. Most men feel like sex more than their wives, and if the wife's not tired or sick or anything, then mostly—if she wants the marriage to be a happy one—she gives him what he wants.'

'But does she have to pretend she likes it as well?'

'You mean fake orgasm?'

Gemma cringed a little. How awful that sounded. Luckily Melanie swept on without her having to say anything further.

'I dare say there aren't too many wives—or women— who haven't faked it at some time or another. But I think, if the relationship is good between husband and wife, she shouldn't have to. Her husband should understand that she's not a machine, and he should be damned grateful that she's giving him satisfaction while not getting any herself. Unfortunately, sometimes a man's ego gets in the way. He takes it as a personal insult if he can't satisfy his wife every time. He might even think that she's stopped loving him, which is crazy.'

'That's one of the reasons I pretended last night,' Gemma admitted unhappily.

Melanie stared at her, clearly astonished.

'I . . . I was upset,' Gemma elaborated with an embarrassed shrug. 'And tired. Nathan wanted to make love and I just couldn't feel anything. He started getting a little rough and he . . . he frightened me, so I . . . I . . . pretended.'

'Bastard,' Melanie hissed, black eyes blazing with fury. 'That was tantamount to rape, Gemma. Can't you see that?'

Gemma was startled by Melanie's fierce words. She instinctively shrank from thinking what Nathan had done was even *close* to rape. 'No, it wasn't,' she denied hotly. 'He . . . he's my husband!'

'God in heaven, does that give him the right to take you by force?'

'No, of course not, but he wouldn't have been expecting me not to like it, and I think he was upset too,' she argued, worried now that she was asking advice from the wrong person. She'd never realised before how much Melanie hated men. She wasn't even *trying* to see Nathan's point of view.

'You shouldn't have to pretend,' Melanie muttered. 'You shouldn't have to squash your own feelings in favour of his all the time. You're right to envy Jade and Kyle. The ideal relationship *is* a partnership in every way. A woman has to have her own individual identity besides being a wife, otherwise, in the end, the husband loses all respect for her. He thinks he can do as he pleases. He thinks he's all powerful. Give a man that sense of power and God knows what terrible things might happen.'

Gemma stared at Melanie, at the passion in her voice—and the hidden anguish. Dear heaven, what had happened in that marriage of hers?

Melanie must have seen the way Gemma was looking at her, for suddenly she seemed to forcibly gather herself, adopting one of those cool calm faces she was famous for. 'Sorry. I was getting carried away. There's no blueprint for marital happiness, Gemma. It's pretty much a play-it-by-ear arrangement. What works for one couple might not work for another. But there's always a period of adjustment before a man and woman really understand each other. Of course it would help if you and Nathan talked things out more. Now drink up that coffee and get a couple of those biscuits into yourself.'

Gemma did just that, endeavouring to see things in a more logical, less emotional way. She'd been making mountains out of molehills, she decided. So Nathan was a bit over-possessive and over-protective. So what? That showed how much he loved her, didn't it? She would go home and cook him a lovely dinner, saying she'd prefer to stay home tonight and just be with him—alone. She'd chill his favorite wine and put on some of his favourite music, or maybe the television. Then, while they were stretched out on the sofa, she might take a bit more of the initiative in lovemaking. She might even . . .

A delicate shudder rippled through Gemma. No, not that. She couldn't do that just yet.

'You should come and visit more often,' Melanie suggested as they walked together to the front door. 'The house is so empty now. I know Byron gets lonely sometimes. And so does Ava.'

'And you, Melanie? Don't you get lonely?'

'Occasionally.'

'Would you go out with Mr Grantham, if he asked you?'

'On a date, you mean?'

'Yes.'

'Never in a million years.'

'Why not?' she asked while she retrieved her suede jacket and slid into it.

'Because I don't like him.'

'I could have sworn you did. Last night you . . . you . . .'

Melanie actually blushed as she had blushed during the dinner party. Now Gemma was *certain* the other woman had found the Englishman attractive.

'He has undeniable sex appeal,' Melanie conceded stiffly, pulling open the front door to let in some watery winter sun. 'But far too much ego. I don't like egocentric men.'

'I wasn't suggesting you *marry* the man, Melanie,' Gemma said with mild exasperation.

Their eyes locked for a second before Melanie answered, 'I'll keep that in mind.'

'So you will go out with him if he asks you?'

'Oh, go on with you.' Melanie practically pushed her out on to the front patio. 'Go home and don't do anything your mother would be ashamed of. Oh! Speaking of your mother, has that private investigator come up with anything?'

'Not a darned thing. It's so hard to get anything out of people at Lightning Ridge. They're naturally suspicious and secretive. As far as the public records are concerned, neither my father nor my mother officially exist. Dad never even filed a tax return. The only place he could be officially found was in the Department of Transport files—his driver's licence and registration of his old truck. But even then he used false documents for ID. I told Nathan not to bother spending any more money for now.'

'What a shame.'

'Nathan says it's all for the best, of course. He says some people's pasts are best left there.'

'Really? Well, I suppose I might be forced to agree with him on that score,' Melanie said drily.

'I don't. It's a horribly empty feeling not knowing who your mother was, or her real name, or what she was like. I haven't given up hope yet. One day soon, I'll go back to Lightning Ridge and see what I can find out myself. I might do better than a stranger.'

'That's true.'

'I'd better go. Thanks for everything, Melanie. I feel much better having talked to you.'

'I'm not sure I helped much.'

'Oh, you have. Bye for now.' Waving, she tripped down the steps and climbed into her new white sedan, a recent present from Nathan. Recalling this—and all the other presents he kept giving her—brought a soft smile to her lips. Nathan loved her. How could she ever have doubted that? Gemma drove home, determined never to doubt her husband's love again.

CHAPTER SEVEN

WHEN Melanie had asked Royce to pick her up at her brother's house at eight, she assumed she would have the place to herself. Ron took Frieda down to the local Workers' Club every Saturday night without fail, leaving the house around six-thirty and never returning till after ten. They only had the one child, a son, Wayne, who was nineteen and very good-looking.

According to Frieda he spent every weekend at his girlfriend's house, much to the girlfriend's mother's annoyance. But when Melanie drove up shortly before seven, planning to leave a note for Ron and Frieda which said she had to go to a school reunion near by and did they mind if she stayed the night, she was confronted by her nephew, very much at home, tinkering with one of his infernal motorbikes on the front porch.

'Damn,' she muttered under her breath.

Wayne looked up as she pushed open the squeaky front gate. 'Oh, hi, there, Aunt Mel,' he said. 'What are you doing here? You do know the oldies are down the club, don't you?'

'Yes, Wayne, but I needed to get a dress I left here. I...I'm going out.' Actually, Melanie kept all her old clothes here, the ones she'd worn as Mrs. Joel Lloyd. She'd lived here with Ron and Frieda for some time after her breakdown, in the bedroom she'd grown up in. This was the Foster family home, Ron having inherited it after their parents passed away in quick succession several years back.

Melanie had been dismayed at being left nothing in the will except her mother's personal effects, but her father had been the last to go and he'd held old-fashioned views about men and women. Melanie, who was nearly twenty years younger than her brother—she'd been a change-of-life baby—had always been treated as an inferior being, her father believing women had no real worth except as wives and mothers.

She sometimes wondered if she had subconsciously absorbed this none too subtle brainwashing, for she'd given up work after her marriage, despite being terribly bored at home till she learnt to fill her days with classes that turned her into a social hostess and housewife the envy of every woman and man in the advertising set around Sydney. It had been these skills that had qualified her for the role of housekeeper at Belleview, a job which she did with ease and total efficiency.

Thinking about her marriage to Joel brought a bitter taste to Melanie's mouth and she dragged her mind back to the present, where Wayne was following her inside, clearly having found a welcome distraction for his own boredom.

'You're really going out, Aunt Mel?' he was saying as he traipsed after her right into her bedroom, draping his none too clean self all over the floral-quilted bed. 'The oldies *will* be pleased. Where are you going?'

'For goodness sakes, get off that bedspread, you grub!' she exploded, avoiding a direct answer. 'Your mother will kill you if you get grease on it!' Frieda was a very particular woman who fussed a lot over the house.

Wayne grudgingly hauled himself off the bed and sprawled on to the chair in the corner. 'Don't start getting like Mum, Aunt Mel,' he grumbled, which brought Melanie up short.

Melanie liked her sister-in-law, who'd been very kind to her after the accident, but she did have some irritating ways. Melanie's brother was his father's son and had typically married a woman who was a professional housewife and who wouldn't dream of having an opinion that didn't match her husband's.

Melanie was aware she'd been much the same with Joel. It was only in hindsight that she realised what a mistake it was for a woman to bury her own personality and identity like that, how it only led to an eventual breaking point. Even Frieda had had a small crisis about a year ago, stunning Ron when she left him for a few days, saying she would come back if he started taking her out at least once a week. Hence their Saturday nights at the club.

Melanie's mind flashed to Gemma and her visit that morning. Hopefully, the girl had enough common sense and spirit to buck Nathan's attempts to rein her into being that sort of meek and mild submissive wife.

'Mum never lets up,' Wayne continued to grumble. 'It's always "Wayne, don't touch that", or "Wayne, don't sit there!"'

Melanie smiled at her nephew, seeing both points of view. 'Come now, Wayne, you do get pretty messy working with those bikes of yours. Maybe if you could remember to clean up a little before coming into the house.'

'Yeah, maybe.' His sullen face suddenly broke into a cheeky grin. 'I guess you'd be just as bad if I came into that big fancy house you look after with grease all over me.'

'You'd better believe it.' Still, Melanie understood now why he spent every weekend at his girlfriend's house. To avoid the nagging.

'Why aren't you at your girlfriend's tonight?' she asked, turning to open the wardrobe and start searching through the dresses. In a way, it was good to have Wayne here. It stopped her nerves from taking over.

'We're having a break,' he said.

'Oh? Is that your idea or her idea?'

'Hers,' he sighed.

'Why do you think she wants a break?'

'Dunno, really. She says it's because I take her for granted.'

'And do you?'

'I guess so.'

Melanie found the red dress she was looking for and turned to face her nephew. 'Have you been sleeping with her?'

Wayne went bright red. 'Gee, Aunt Mel...'

'*Have* you?'

'Well...sure! Everyone does these days. You...you won't tell Mum and Dad, will you?'

'Wayne, do you honestly think they don't know? Don't take the oldies for fools. I hope you've been using protection,' she warned, her stomach turning over as she thought of what she had bought on the way over here. And what was lying in the bottom drawer of the dressing-table in this very room.

'Course,' he muttered. 'I'm not stupid, you know.'

'It's stupid to do something just because everyone's doing it. Making love should be special, Wayne, with someone you really love and care about. It should...' She broke off, guilt and shame consuming her. Who am I to lecture anyone on matters of sex, tonight of all nights?

'Wayne, I really must get ready,' she said brusquely. 'My date is going to be here at eight and it's already gone seven.'

'OK.' He levered his six-foot frame out of the chair. 'Am I allowed to ask where you're going?'

'To dinner. In the city,' she added curtly. 'Now out!'

'OK, OK, don't get your dander up. Gee, Aunt Mel, a date, eh?' His eyes swept over her as if wondering what man would want to take out his drab, thirty-two-year-old Aunt Mel. Shrugging, he left the room, shutting the door behind him.

By five to eight, Melanie had been reduced to a quivering mess. She'd already poked herself in the eye with her mascara wand and smudged her nail polish—twice! But at last, she was ready.

Standing back, she surveyed her reflection in the mirror, hardly recognising the woman who stared back at her. She'd been so used to seeing herself as Wayne saw her, drab and dreary. What on earth had Royce seen in her yesterday to make him want her? He could have his pick of women.

The woman in the mirror, however, would turn any man's head. This was the woman Joel had created, and displayed. Vibrant and vivacious and yes...sensual.

The red woollen dress with its low scooped neckline and long tight sleeves hugged her womanly curves down to her voluptuous hips, where it flared out into a softly gored skirt falling to mid-calf. Delicate black sandals with ankle-straps had replaced her normal chunky black shoes, silken sheer stockings in barely black caressing her shapely legs instead of her usual thick beige ones.

Red suited her colouring, bringing a warm glow to her fair skin and highlighting her blue-black hair which was no longer up, but falling in its natural lush waves to her shoulders from a side-parting, sweeping slightly over her left eye. Her black eyes were strikingly made up with plenty of black eyeliner and mascara, her generous mouth filled in with a scarlet gloss that matched her dress—as did her nail polish. She'd put blusher on her cheeks, despite not needing any. Her colour was high tonight, as her pulse-rate was high, riding on fear more than desire, nerves rather than courage.

Where is that new Melanie when I need her most? she asked her reflection.

Wayne simultaneously knocked and burst into her room. 'Aunt Mel, a black...' He broke off in mid-sentence to stare at his aunt who'd swung round at his sudden entrance, the red skirt flaring before settling into more sedate folds around her legs. Wayne's stunned gaze swept up from those legs to her face. 'My God,' he whispered on a low, shocked note. 'I...I...'

Melanie's smile was wry. 'You were saying, Wayne?'

Her nephew walked forward to survey her further, shaking his head. 'Aunt Mel, you're...you're *gorgeous*!'

She had to laugh. 'Your words are complimentary, nephew, dear, but your expression isn't.'

Wayne didn't have the grace to look embarrassed. 'Well, you're usually so...so...' Now he was really at a loss for words.

'Plain?' Melanie suggested.

'No, not exactly plain...' His face screwed up into a puzzled frown.

'Never mind, Wayne, what was it you wanted to tell me?'

His face cleared and brightened. 'Oh, yes, I think your date's arrived. In a black Ferrari, no less.'

'A what? Never mind, I heard.' Could one hire a Ferrari? She supposed so. But if he'd arrived, why hadn't he blown the horn?

Her answer to that came when the front doorbell rang.

'I'll get it, Aunt Mel,' Wayne immediately offered, and was gone before she could stop him.

'Damn, damn and double damn,' Melanie muttered. Wayne was sure to recognise Royce. Her nephew was a racing car nut! Things were going from bad to worse.

Melanie breathed in then let out a ragged sigh. She should have known she wasn't cut out for this kind of thing. Her stomach was in instant knots. Her heart was racing, and her palms were clammy.

Wayne soon reappeared in the doorway, looking stunned. 'Aunt Mel! You...you do realise who it is you're going out with tonight, don't you?'

Melanie sighed again. 'Yes, Wayne, I do. It's Royce Grantham.'

'But it's...*the* Royce Grantham. You know?'

'Yes, that's right. *The* Royce Grantham, the Formula One driver.'

'God.' He stared at her with awe in his gaze. 'Fancy that. Royce Grantham, taking out *my* aunt. Wait till I tell my mates. Wait till I tell Mum and Dad. They'll be wrapped!'

Melanie opened her mouth to implore Wayne not to tell anyone then shut it again. Suddenly, the new Melanie swept back in, bringing her a lifted chin and renewed defiance. They might as well know that change was on the way. After all, Royce might be the first man she'd gone out with in four years, but he wasn't going to be the last. Once Royce had gone back to England there would be more dates with more men. Even the old Melanie couldn't bear to look at the rest of her life with no outings and no male company. The new Melanie wasn't going to do without sex, either.

Still, no point in Wayne giving Ron and Frieda false hopes.

'It's only a date, Wayne,' she reminded him drily. 'I met Royce last night at Belleview and he's a stranger to Sydney. I said I'd show him the sights of the city on a Saturday night. Now, where have you put him?'

'He wouldn't come in. He's waiting on the front porch.'

'Did you introduce yourself?'

'I sure did. There's no flies on me!'

'And what do you think of him?' she asked as she put a few things into the black beaded evening bag she'd selected earlier.

'What do I think of him?' Wayne looked perplexed. 'What's to think, Aunt Mel? He's Royce Grantham, for Pete's sake!'

Melanie suddenly understood what Kyle had been talking about last night when he said rich men had a real problem finding a woman to love them for themselves. The rich and *famous*, she decided, had double trouble. People were blinded, not only by their money, but by their aura of success. Maybe that was why Royce had never married, because he lived in an artificial environment where people were automatically impressed without even knowing him. That could be a very corrupting way to live.

'Ready, Aunt Mel?' Wayne asked agitatedly. 'He's waiting, you know.'

'Well, let him wait!' she snapped, annoyed with herself for starting to think of Royce as a real person with real problems to contend with. She only wanted to think of him as a male body.

Such thinking was back on track once she sighted him standing there under the light of the front porch. He looked lethally attractive in a grey woollen suit, with a sexy black T-shirt where another man would have put a stuffy shirt and tie. Suddenly, her stomach curled over and, while some deeply embedded instinct kept warning her to run as far away from this man as she could, her body had ideas of its own.

Wayne was hot on her heels as she walked down the corridor, so Melanie stopped for a second and hissed over her shoulder for him to get lost.

'Aunt Mel,' he groaned. 'Don't be a spoil-sport.'

'Wayne, I mean it,' she said darkly.

'Yeah...right...OK. Have a good time. Don't do anything I wouldn't do,' he muttered as he loped off, back in the direction of the kitchen.

I won't, Wayne, Melanie thought with black humour, and, taking a steadying breath, continued the long walk to the front door, aware that Royce was staring at her as much as she was staring at him.

'I thought I told you not to come in,' she said straight away, her voice a little strangled with nerves. Did he like the way she looked or not? Why was he frowning at her as though he was a psychiatrist and she was his trickiest patient?

'Mr Hyde, I presume?' he mocked, ignoring her complaint and letting those sexy blue eyes of his sweep over her once more.

'Mr Hyde?' she repeated thickly, aware of little but the lump in her throat and the mad thudding of her heart against her ribs.

'As in Jekyll and Hyde.'

The analogy shocked her for a second till she accepted it had some essence of truth in it. She was distracted and disappointed, however, by his not directly complimenting her appearance. 'Are you saying you don't like how I look?'

'Do you think I'm crazy? You're absolutely stunning. Shall we go?'

He took her elbow and guided her quickly down the front steps and out to the pavement where a black sports car was indeed parked behind her small grey sedan.

'Wayne tells me this is a Ferrari,' she remarked as Royce opened the passenger door and stepped back to wave her inside.

'If it isn't,' he said drily while she folded herself into the low-slung seat, 'then I know a certain car rental agency that's going to get sued.'

He slammed the door shut and strode around to slip in behind the large steering wheel. Melanie couldn't quite make out his mood. Was he angry with her? If so, why? He was getting what he wanted, wasn't he?

'I think you, of all people,' she said, agitation making her voice sharp, 'would know a Ferrari when you saw one.'

'True. I drove for them once. They say all Formula One drivers should drive for Ferrari at least once, so that they're damned glad to get back to driving for someone else!'

'If they're so difficult to drive for, then why do it at all?'

'For the money. What else? So where are we off to, sweet Melanie? Dinner and dancing? A movie, perhaps? A romantic stroll under the moonlight? You forgot to tell me while you were delivering your orders last night exactly what was expected of me after I'd honked.'

His hypocritic sarcasm sparked a surge of anger, which she just managed to keep under control by clenching her teeth hard in her jaw.

'But you didn't honk, did you?' she bit out.

'No. Funny, that. I have a natural aversion to following orders.'

'Then why ask me for more? Oh, just drive straight to your hotel, Royce. I'm not in the mood for games.'

'Really? From what I can see,' he said, eyes raking over her hair and face, 'your whole damned life is one big game. Talk about Dr Jekyll and Mr Hyde.'

'Just drive, damn you!' she spat, glaring at him.

He glared right back for a long moment, before reefing his eyes away and firing the engine. 'Put your seatbelt on,' he ordered curtly. 'You're going to need it.'

That was the understatement of the year.

The Ferrari screeched round in a savage U-turn and careered down to the corner where without hesitation it swept out on to busy Parramatta Road. There was no doubting Royce's skill as they darted in and out of the trucks and cars, changing lanes, overtaking, braking and accelerating with heart-stoppingly small margins for error. After five minutes of sheer terror, Melanie's nerve broke.

'If you don't slow down,' she cried out, 'I'll grab that wheel and to hell with the consequences.'

Royce said nothing, making her gasp again in fright as he wrenched the wheel left, just missing a car, then lurched round a corner on squealing tyres before screeching over to the kerb and braking to a shuddering halt.

'You stupid bastard!' she flung over at him, her face still flaming with surges of fear-filled adrenalin. 'How dare you drive like that around city streets? How dare you risk my life and others in such a pathetic display of schoolboy arrogance! What did you think you were proving by hurtling around in this elongated tin can like you were driving in a Grand Prix? That it made you into more of a man?'

Melanie had little time to register the dangerous glitter in those hard blue eyes. Neither did she have any chance to extricate herself from her low-slung prison before Royce swiftly unsnapped his seatbelt, swivelled and loomed over her. There was the fleeting impression of a whooshing sound, of the scent of expensive after-shave, of a darkened face overhead, and then all there was were his hands capturing her face, his mouth prising hers open, his tongue, driving deep.

Melanie moaned beneath the onslaught, her already heated blood quickly changing from anger to arousal. And with the change came a passion even she had not envisaged. It took possession of her body with a vengeance, making it throb as the still running engine beneath her feet was throbbing.

Hard wild kisses followed with even harder, wilder kisses. Soon, Melanie's lips felt raw and swollen. When Royce ran his wet tongue over them, she trembled. When he sucked each lip in turn into his mouth, she groaned at the bittersweet sensations.

'You drive me wild,' he muttered huskily. 'Do you know that? Touch me, Melanie. Touch me...'

Her hands parted his jacket and ran over the black T-shirt, his chest muscles well-defined beneath the thin material. She could feel his chest wall rising and falling rapidly, feel his sharp inward breath whenever her fingers found a male nipple. His response to her touch excited her unbearably and her impassioned fingers travelled downwards till he gasped, then groaned, then grabbed her hands.

'No,' he growled. 'Not here. And not like that.'

She stared up at him, eyes glazed, no cohesive thought in her head. Her eyes blazed with a blind passion, wanting nothing but to have this man make love to her. Her yearnings burnt within her hot black gaze, telling him she was his in whatever way he wanted her. For a second he stared at her, as though disbelieving of this wicked new Melanie. Disbelieving, yet fascinated.

'Hell,' he muttered under his breath, then, shaking his head, sagged back into his seat. Another sideways glance betrayed a continuing bewilderment. 'Who are you, Melanie Lloyd? *What* are you? No, don't answer. I don't think I want to know.'

Firing the engine, he negotiated a much safer U-turn and headed once again in the direction of the city.

Melanie sank back into her seat, her eyes closing as the confusing reality of what had just happened settled into some order in her mind. Unbelievably, it seemed Royce was able to arouse her much more quickly and intensely than Joel. She also seemed to want him even more than she had ever wanted Joel.

Now that didn't seem right. She'd loved Joel This... this was just a sexual thing. Superficial and shallow, with no depth of feeling or caring. Yet it had sent her spiralling out of control, made her ready to do anything to please him. That wasn't right. It just wasn't right.

Melanie frowned, trying to make sense of it.

Maybe it's because I'm older, she decided. She'd read that women reached their sexual prime much later than men. And she had to be extra frustrated, not having been with a man in years. Yes, that had to be it. For what else could it be?

A shocking thought had her slanting a panicky glance over at Royce, at his ruggedly handsome face and his long strong hands, gripping the wheel with white-knuckled intensity. As if sensing her eyes upon him, his head jerked around, but she quickly looked away afraid of what *he* might see, afraid of what *she* might feel.

It can't be, she told herself shakily. I don't believe it. I won't believe it! It's just sex. Nothing more. I can't cope with anything more!

Gradually, she calmed, common sense telling her that she was merely trying to justify what she was doing. That was all. This was her first venture into a strictly sexual affair, her first foray into lust. Next time, she decided with a twisting of her heart, it would be easier.

CHAPTER EIGHT

THE Regency Hotel was one of the newest in Sydney, nestled in a side-street down towards the Quay, where all the rooms could have a view of the harbour. The atmosphere and décor was rich and plush, with lots of wood-panelled walls and velvet curtains and gold fittings, reminiscent of some of the older, ritzier London hotels.

Royce's suite—Melanie told herself she should have guessed he'd have a suite—was on the tenth floor, and comprised an elegant sitting- and dining-room in peach and green, which led discreetly to a master bedroom in the same colours, off which came a sumptuous bathroom which went for broke in cream marble with gold taps. Fresh flowers sat in the corners of the triple vanity and the shower alone would have housed six people.

Melanie had tried to settle her nerves on arrival with a visit to the bathroom, where she replenished her lipstick and combed her hair, all the while desperately battling to find a suitable façade to get her through the coming ordeal. But, much as she tried to summon up the new Melanie, she continued to elude her. Instead, all she could find was a brittle sarcasm to shore up her imminent disintegration.

'You like to live well, Royce, don't you?' she said drily on exiting the bathroom after trying out the toilet and matching bidet. Nerves always did have an unfortunate effect on her bladder.

He was standing in the bedroom doorway, watching her with a thoughtful expression on his face. 'I've earned it,' he said.

'You're lucky you've lived to spend it,' she flung at him, 'the way you drive.'

93

He laughed and turned to disappear back into the sitting-room. 'Come out here and have a drink with me?' he called out. 'I think we both need it.'

'I don't usually drink,' she said on joining him, sitting down on one of the low green linen sofas and placing her purse on the coffee-table. 'But I think you're right,' she went on ruefully. 'I certainly could do with one.'

He shot her a puzzled look, then shrugged and turned to open the cabinet that housed the mini-bar and bar fridge. 'What shall we have? Scotch?'

'Whatever,' came her taut reply.

She didn't watch as he poured the drinks, feigning an interest in the view afforded by the floor to ceiling windows on her right. She'd never seen the Opera House framed by peach velvet curtains before, but she supposed it looked as spectacular as ever with its incredible roof of interlocking sails. From this height and at night, surrounded by darkly lapping waters, it really stood out. As did the Quay area, lit for the tourists all year round. But in truth, Sydney harbour and the postcard beauty of its surroundings couldn't distract her from her growing agitation.

Melanie's relief when Royce handed her a glass then settled himself on the sofa opposite showed itself in a deep sigh. The coffee-table between them provided an adequate barrier to his touching her in any way, even her foot. Why the idea of his touching her filled her with such alarm all of a sudden she couldn't fathom. One would have thought that would have been what she wanted. After all, once he started making love to her she would probably forget everything else, as she had in the car.

Which reminded her. She had to discuss certain matters with him.

Shifting nervously on the sofa, she recrossed her legs and stared at the view some more. The sensible words she should have been saying just wouldn't come.

'You haven't done this type of thing before, have you?' Royce said abruptly, but with an odd note of surprise in his voice.

It brought her eyes round with a jerk. 'Why
say it like that?' A frown drew her dark brows toge
'Did... did you think I had?'

His laugh was sardonic. 'After last night's phone call.
What do you think I thought?'

'Oh...' An embarrassed heat flooded her face at the
realisation that she must have sounded like the toughest
old tart in the world. Lifting the glass to her lips, she
took a deep swallow before spluttering and grimacing
down at the amber liquid.

'You didn't want it straight?' he asked. 'Here, give it
back to me and I'll add some soda. Or would you prefer
ginger ale?'

'No...' She shook her head. 'No, it's all right.'

'Are you hungry? Would you like me to order some
supper from Room Service?'

She stared at him. 'Why... why are you being so nice
to me?' she croaked.

He seemed startled by her question. 'What did you
expect? That I would rip off your clothes the moment
I shut the door and ravish you on the floor?'

Her eyes dropped. 'I... I don't know. Maybe it would
have been better if you had.' Her voice sounded bitter
yet all she was feeling was a black emptiness. 'It's what
you brought me here for, after all.' She gulped some
more whisky then placed the glass on the coffee-table
with a shaking hand, unknowing that the eyes she lifted
held a haunted look that would have moved the hardest
of hearts.

'No, Melanie,' Royce denied in a low, measured voice.
'Maybe that's all *you* came here for, but that's not the
way I do things with women I really like. I'll order us
some supper. Do you like seafood?' He stood up and
she had to crink her neck to look up at him.

'I... yes, yes, I do.'

'Good.' His smile was far too sweet and she quickly
dropped her eyes again, hiding her fluster by picking up
the glass again and sipping the rest of her drink. But
while her ears automatically listened to him moving over
to the phone on the desk in the corner behind her, where

o order a platter of seafood, crusty rolls,
d fresh strawberries, her mind was

ng him too much, she realised. Far too
s not what she wanted, for it made her
and vulnerable. This wasn't supposed to
be a warm romantic encounter, simply a sexual one.

'Can I get you another drink?' he asked on returning.
'Or will you wait for the champagne?'

'I'll wait,' she said tautly.

'Then so will I.'

As he settled back down on the sofa, she said abruptly,
'I want you to use protection. If you don't have any I've
brought some with me.'

His silent stare unnerved her.

'I . . . I *am* protected against pregnancy,' she went on
agitatedly, 'but there are so many other risks these days,
risks not covered by . . . by . . .'

'I will use protection, Melanie,' he agreed, 'though I
am not one of those risks.'

'I only have your word for that, though, don't I?' she
snapped.

'You do.' His tone was quite cold. 'I presume my word
holds little value for you?'

'I have learnt not to trust the word of men like you,'
she returned just as coldly.

'You know, Melanie, that's the second time you've
used that phrase in connection with me. What kind of
man is a man like me? Are you referring to the fact that
I'm a so-called swinging bachelor, or something even
less savoury?'

'Let's just say I'm not convinced of your honour or
sincerity where women are concerned. You tried to pick
me up that first day, Royce, without even knowing me.
I suspect you might have brought me straight up here,
if I'd let you.'

There was no escaping the guilt that flashed across his
face. 'Probably,' he confessed. 'But it's not my usual
style. Yours was an unusual case, Melanie Lloyd.'

'I don't see how,' she remarked with contempt in her voice.

'I'm not sure I do either, but it's true. Still, I can see I have little chance of convincing you that I've never felt anything as powerful as what I felt on seeing you yesterday.'

'It's called lust, Royce. L-U-S-T,' she spelled out sharply. 'Though frankly, I'm not sure how I could have inspired *anything* yesterday. I looked like a dog.'

His laughter broke the angry tension that was developing between them. 'You could never look like a dog, Melanie. Unless you're talking about a sleek pedigreed variety. You have lines that no clothes could hide, and a face only a master could do justice to.'

Melanie didn't want to feel pleasure at his extravagant compliments, but she was doomed to failure. Her cheeks pinked and she hastily looked down into her lap lest he see her vulnerability. It was to be thanked that she was sitting down for she suspected her knees had just gone to water.

'Why don't you come over here and join me?' Royce murmured. 'You're too far away.'

'You're the one who sat over there,' she countered, her eyes snapping up in rebellion against her moment of weakness. 'Why don't you come over here?'

His grin showed her the ease with which she'd just trapped herself. 'I thought you'd never ask.'

God, but he was a quick mover, over beside her and drawing her into his arms before she could say Jack Robinson.

'No, I...' was all she got out before his lips closed over hers and the room around them receded.

Somehow her arms ended up around him under his jacket and she was pulling him closer and closer, the urge to remove all air between their bodies as compulsive as the urge to have his tongue drive deeper and deeper into her mouth.

The sound of a knock on the door had them gasping apart, Melanie's black eyes wildly dilated as she stared into Royce's equally stunned face. Both his hands lifted to rake his now dishevelled brown hair back from his forehead, a wry smile curving his rather cruel mouth as he surveyed her swollen lips.

'Have I got lipstick all over me?' he asked.

'Yes . . .'

He nodded. 'In that case, *you* answer the door while I pay a visit to the bathroom. Or aren't you liberated enough to reverse roles?' he mocked lightly.

A giggle escaped her lips before she could stop it. But his words about reversed roles had sent an image into her mind, a very sexy image of her on top.

'Melanie Lloyd,' he said teasingly, 'that was a very naughty giggle. I'll want to know what brought it on when I get back.'

Kissing her cheek, he was gone, leaving her to do as he asked and answer the door.

'Good evening, madam,' the waiter greeted her, then wheeled in their supper on a trolley-style serving table. When he went to remove the covers on the food, she told him just to leave it. When he started formally setting the dining-table, she told him to leave that as well. Frowning, then shrugging, he wished her a pleasant evening, gave a small bow and left, closing the door quietly behind him.

Royce rejoined her without his jacket, and what she'd thought was a black T-shirt actually had long sleeves. Most men looked sexy in black, she conceded. Royce, however, looked dangerous as well. She found it impossible to stop her eyes from coveting his broadshouldered, lean torso as he walked towards her.

'Mmm,' he said, his arms snaking around her waist to draw her hard against him. 'You can look at me like that any time you like. Now kiss me, wench, and make it good. I've already forgotten what you taste like.'

She kissed him. And then *he* kissed *her*, and soon it was clear that any eating was going to be postponed. Royce found the zip at the back of the dress, swearing when his efforts to rid her of her clothing were hampered by the tightness of the long sleeves. Several savage tugs later, the dress pooled at her feet while he attacked her bra, only to swear again.

'It's a front-opening clasp,' she told him shakily, her bones having melted to mush. He whirled her in his arms and she sank back into him while he fumbled and fiddled, still swearing.

'I always have trouble with black lace bras,' he growled. 'They do things to me.'

Finally, the bra fell apart under his fingers and Melanie groaned aloud. But oh, the feel of his hands on her bare breasts.

'Royce...'

'Shut up, Melanie, I'm enjoying myself.'

She whimpered her own pleasure as he teased her nipples into hard pebbles of the most exquisite sensitivity. At last, he turned her round and swept her up into his arms, laying her down on the nearest sofa then kneeling down beside it and bending to delight her breasts further with his mouth. He seemed to know just when she wanted him to lick her softly, when to suck a little more firmly, when to nip and bite till she was beside herself. Then and only then did his hands move to peel her tights and black lace briefs down her legs, though once again he found an impediment to his progress in the guise of the ankle-straps of her sandals. Some more swearing followed—quite colourful really—and she laughed.

'You won't be laughing soon,' he warned darkly.

And she wasn't.

The shoes and undergarments finally discarded, he started working his way back up her legs, kissing her, licking her, caressing her, past her calves, her knees, her thighs. When he pushed one of her legs off the sofa, then raised the knee of the other, she was beyond protest. A soft moan was all she could manage as his fingers and tongue started to work in unison.

Melanie's hands lifted to fall across her eyes which were squeezing tight in an effort to stop her body from doing what Royce seemed intent on making it do. Her heart was beating faster and faster and everything inside her was twisting tighter and tighter. She wanted to cry out for him to stop but suddenly her pleasure burst like a mini-explosion and her back arched, her mouth gasping wide for air. The spasms seemed to last forever and by the time her heavy arms finally slumped away from her eyes, one falling limply over the edge of the sofa, she was feeling totally drained.

'She liked that, methinks,' Royce chuckled softly and her eyes fluttered open to find him still kneeling beside her but rapidly stripping. His black sweater was reefed over his head to reveal a lean-muscled chest with a triangle of dark curls in the centre. She smiled in languorous amusement when he sat down on the floor and wriggled out of his trousers and underwear, amazing herself when she reached out without hesitation to stroke his beautiful erection.

'God, Melanie,' he protested at last. 'Don't keep doing that. I'm a man, not a machine. Besides, I have to go and get something.'

'Open my bag,' she ordered huskily. 'Behind you, on the coffee-table.'

He twisted round and did, his eyes flinging wide. 'Good God, how many did you buy?'

She blushed prettily. 'They... they were cheaper by the dozen.'

'Thank heaven for small mercies. For a minute there I thought you were expecting me to use the lot! Now there's a thought.' He grinned over his shoulder at her as he ripped one of the packages open. 'Maybe I could look upon this as a new challenge. Damn, do you think I could have some help here?' he asked, turning back to her without the slightest embarrassment. 'I'm all fingers and thumbs thinking of my new challenge.' And he pressed the condom into her hand.

She gave a low, husky laugh. 'Well, we can't have that, can we?' But once she started to do what he asked, her throat went dry and her own fingers started shaking. Even so, they kept caressing him long after the task was completed. And he let her, urging her to use her mouth as well, to pleasure him as he had pleasured her. Stunned a little at first, she did what he wanted, surprised when she found a pleasure in it that she never had when Joel had coerced her into such intimacies.

Maybe it was because of the way Royce was touching her while she did it. Stroking her hair so tenderly, all the while telling her that what she was doing felt fantastic, that she was incredibly sexy and ravishingly beautiful and that he adored her.

'Enough,' he murmured at last, and tenderly lifted her into a sitting position in front of him, stroking her thighs apart and bending forward to kiss her on the mouth while his fingers caressed her open for him. Melanie was all heat and liquid by the time he eased himself into her, but still, her eyes flung wide at the feel of his flesh fusing with hers.

'Royce,' she moaned softly.

'Hush. Don't talk. Put your arms around my neck.'

She did so, gasping when he cupped her buttocks and lifted her forward so that his penetration was even deeper.

'Now kiss me,' he urged thickly.

She kissed him. And it was while her own tongue was sliding in and out of his mouth that he began an almost parallel rhythm with his own lower body, quickly taking her to a place where nothing else existed but his flesh inside hers, and the slow-building tension gripping every internal muscle she owned. Soon, her hips began to pump in response to his movements, her mouth was gasping away from his, and she was giving voice to her need in hot, wild words. Her nails dug into his neck and she felt herself reaching for release once more.

It came like a volcano, bursting upwards through her, making her cry out in shock at the stunning nature of her pleasure. For it was not just sexual. It was a complete experience, both physical and emotional, especially when she heard Royce's answering cries of satisfaction. God, but she'd never felt anything like it. Not ever. Their bodies pulsating as one, meeting each other's needs, sharing in each other's pleasure.

She clung to him, raining kisses on his neck and shoulders, telling him that he was the best lover in the whole wide world. In reply, he held her just as fiercely, rocking her slowly back and forth as the tempest calmed, allowing her to savour every last sensation, seemingly not wanting it to end any more than she did. She groaned when he finally laid her limp body back on the sofa and deserted her for a while, her eyes and limbs growing heavy as all the energy drained from her satiated flesh. She was lying there, half asleep, and feeling deliciously languid, when a still naked Royce loomed over her, dry amusement on his face.

'Oh, no,' he laughed. 'This will never do.'

Scooping her up, he carried her through the bedroom and into the shower with him, making her squeal and struggle in his arms under the sudden blast of cold water.

'Wake up, witch,' he growled as he held her ruthlessly beneath the spray. 'I haven't had enough of you yet.'

At long last, the water turned warm and he lowered her spluttering self to her feet, effectively stopping any further protest with another of his highly distracting kisses.

'Hungry now?' he asked thickly after a minute or two.

'For food? Or other things?'

'Both.'

'You're insatiable,' she laughed when his hands started working on her breasts again.

'Just trying to keep the engine running. And well oiled,' he added hoarsely, one hand having found its way down between her legs. 'No trouble there, I see.'

She blushed. 'You're terrible.'

'And you're gorgeous.' Groaning, he pulled her to him for another round of kisses while water cascaded down over them.

'I think we should return to the living-room,' he muttered at last.

'The seafood calls, does it?'

'No. That's where your bag is.'

It was a crazy, incredibly sexy evening, with their making love at regular intervals and in the most adventurous ways, laughing in between, getting drunk on champagne and generally acting like honeymooners. Royce did his level best to meet his new challenge but fell short by three or four. As for Melanie, she adored the way he could spin her into a daze of desire and delight that had no thought of tomorrow or the past or anything. She'd never felt so totally sensual as she did beneath his lips and hands, never so complete as when he drove his body deep inside hers.

They finally made the mistake of making love in the bed, its comfort seducing them to sleep afterwards. The last thing Melanie remembered was telling Royce she had to go home, that it was terribly late, but then she drifted off...

At some time during the night, she roused sufficiently for her sleepy arm to steal round his naked waist and pull him close back to her. She snuggled around him, spoon-fashion, loving the feel of his hard male body. So strong, yet warm and sweet and cuddly. Her lips pressed to his back, his shoulder, his arm. I wish I could do this every night, she thought dreamily. I wish...

Melanie snapped awake, eyes wide. Dear God, what was she doing? No... what had she *done*? There was to have been no feeling, no emotion, no silly *wishing*. Royce was just a body to be used for a while, then discarded afterwards, without afterthought, without pain.

Oh, God, what a fool she was! She'd felt the warning signs, but she hadn't heeded them. She should have known she wouldn't be able to give her body so totally and not be in danger of giving her heart.

Yet the man lying beside her had no use for foolish women's hearts. Oh, he wanted their bodies, as often and in as many varied ways as he could have them. But it was strictly sex on his part. Never anything more. She should have followed his example.

Well, there was only one solution. She had to break with him now, while her feelings still fell short of love. Yes, she would never see him again. Never ever. She would have to be strong, have to resist temptation, have to say no if he asked her out again.

He might not ask you out again anyway, came the added bitter thought. They'd done just about everything last night, everything a man and a woman could do. Whatever sexual challenge she had represented to him had been well and truly met. Whatever fantasy he'd wanted her to fulfil, she had. Besides, one-night stands were called that because they lasted one night. End of story.

Feeling totally wretched, Melanie crept out of the bed and gathered up her clothes, taking them into the bathroom where she dressed quickly and quietly. The sight of towels spread on the floor from one of their encounters jolted her for a moment, but she steadfastly refused to accept shame or guilt. She'd clearly needed sex, needed Royce—the man. What she didn't need, however, was to start needing Royce—the person.

It was just on four when she let herself out of the room. By four-thirty the taxi was dropping her off at home where, thankfully, no one woke up. Not that she didn't creep around like a mouse. She soon tumbled her weary body into bed, where she fell into an exhausted sleep.

CHAPTER NINE

'IT'S about time you got up,' Frieda said accusingly when a yawning, dressing-gown-clad Melanie walked into the kitchen shortly before noon on the Sunday. 'Royce said not to disturb you, that you'd got in rather late, but truly, Melanie, it's very rude to invite a man over for the day then not be out of bed when he arrives. It's also rude not to tell your own family that you've decided to start dating again. You know how pleased we would have been. I can't understand why you kept it a secret.'

Melanie's hand fluttered up to her throat. 'Royce is *here*? *Now*?'

'Well, of course he is! Why look so surprised?' Frieda's face showed irritation. A thin, wiry woman, with sharp features and impatient blue eyes, she moved quickly and spoke quickly, with an easily exasperated manner. 'You told him eleven, didn't you? And it's way past eleven. I wish you'd thought to leave me a note since he'll be here for lunch. As it is, I had to move the roast dinner from tonight to lunchtime. It'll be ready around one-thirty. I hope he likes lamb,' she muttered, and started slicing beans into a saucepan in the sink.

'Where...where is he?' Melanie asked, sitting down at the kitchen table before she fell down.

'Helping Wayne with his bike in the back yard. Seems he knows something about engines.' Frieda glanced up, her expression dry. 'There again, he would, wouldn't he, him being a world champion racing car driver and all?'

'You...you know about that too, do you?' came Melanie's weak comment.

'Hard not to. Wayne was raving on about him to his father and me over breakfast this morning. Not to mention how you looked last night. Done up to the nines, it seems. So what is going on between you and this man,

Melanie? Where did you meet? Are you serious about each other? I still can't understand why you didn't tell us, your own flesh and blood!'

'Goodness, Frieda,' Melanie gasped. 'Don't get so carried away. Didn't Wayne tell you I was simply doing my boss a good turn, showing one of his clients around Sydney while he was here? You do realise Royce is only in Sydney on holiday. And I didn't invite him here for the day. We were supposed to be going out, sightseeing.'

I'll kill him, she was thinking as she desperately tried to extricate herself from this horrible mess.

'That's not the impression he gave me, Melanie,' Frieda countered archly. 'He told me he was fed up with doing the tourist scene and that he was looking forward to spending a day relaxing with a nice normal Australian family with no pretensions. He said you'd told him what a good cook I was and that he couldn't wait to sample an old-fashioned home-cooked meal. He said he had had it up to here...' Melanie blinked as Frieda whipped the bean-slicer up to eye-level '...with hotel food.'

'He did, did he?' Well, that's not the impression *she'd* got when he devoured the seafood platter last night, Melanie thought sourly. But it was a clever manipulative lie trotted out by a rogue intent on having his wicked way with her. *Again.* No doubt he'd woken this morning to find her gone, and—not ready yet to give up such a delicious morsel—he'd set out to secure seconds for himself by fair means or foul.

Melanie sat there, fuming. She should never have let Royce pick her up here. She should have taken a taxi to his hotel and met him there. Now, he'd backed her into a corner from which it would prove difficult to escape.

Difficult, but not impossible. She would simply have to go along with this charade till she could get away from here. And then she would let him have it, right between the eyes. No man backed Melanie Lloyd into corners these days, certainly not a scoundrel like Royce Grantham!

'Melanie, surely you're not going to just sit there in that ghastly old pink dressing-gown,' her sister-in-law berated sternly. 'Royce could come in at any moment and see you like that with no lipstick on and your hair a mess. Go and make yourself presentable immediately!'

Melanie stayed exactly where she was, though she did scoop her hair back from her face, sighing as she did so. 'You haven't been listening to me, Frieda. There is nothing serious between Mr Grantham and myself. Not even remotely! Neither have I put myself on the marriage market again. I've simply decided to date occasionally and, when Royce asked me to show him around the city, I decided why not. Frankly I've been wanting to start going out again for a while, but I don't meet many eligible men at Belleview. Most of Byron's friends are married for starters.'

'Well, he's not any more.'

'Who? Royce? I didn't know he'd ever been married at all!'

'No, not him,' came Frieda's frustrated-sounding reply. 'I was talking about Byron Whitmore.'

Melanie couldn't help showing amazement. 'What are you suggesting, Frieda? That I should actually make a line for Byron?'

Frieda shrugged. 'He's a very handsome man. And very eligible. I think he likes you, too. Remember when we talked you into answering his advertisement for a housekeeper and you said you didn't stand a chance because you had no real experience?'

'Yes. But I don't see...'

'For pity's sake,' Frieda huffed. 'Why do you think he hired you above all the other applicants? Because he liked the *look* of you. Maybe because he was *attracted* to you.'

'Oh, don't be ridiculous, Frieda!' Melanie laughed. 'He hired me because he *wasn't* attracted to me, that's why. That wife of his had an eagle eye when it came to her husband and other women, I can assure you. No, Frieda, you're wrong. Byron hired me for the opposite reason, because he knew I'd be the last woman on earth to make a line for him. Besides,' she added drily, 'he's not my type.'

'Not like your racing car driver, eh?' Frieda suggested with a smirk. 'He's your type, isn't he? Physical, yet clever. Don't look so surprised. I know the sort of man who would attract you, Melanie. A man like Joel. Yes, I saw the similarity right away, but where Joel had a hard, almost ruthless streak in him, Royce is more of a cheeky, naughty boy.'

Melanie stared at her sister-in-law, never having realised she was so intuitive. But she was right, of course. Royce didn't seem to be as ruthless as Joel had proven to be. And he could charm the birds out of the trees when he put his mind to it. But that didn't mean he wasn't a dangerous man to start feeling things for other than the most superficial. He was still a very selfish, conscienceless individual, as evidenced by his coming here today without an invitation. Did he honestly think she would be *pleased* to see him, that she would welcome this intrusion into her private and personal life with open arms? The man was in for a shock if he did.

Unfortunately she wouldn't be able to show her displeasure while the others were around. His ticking-off would have to wait.

'Is Ron out with Royce and Wayne?' she asked, frowning.

'Melanie, where *are* your brains this morning? You know he coaches the under-twelves' soccer team, and that they play a match every Sunday during the winter months. He won't be back till four at the earliest. I'll have to put his dinner on a plate and reheat it. Look, if you're determined not to get dressed yet, why don't you get yourself a cup of coffee?' she went on. 'It might wake up that sleepy head of yours. Still, you must have had a good time last night, if you got home so late.'

'What? Oh, yes . . . yes, it was very nice.'

'Royce is nice too. I have to admit I was pleasantly surprised by him. You rather expect the rich and famous to be stuck up, but he's very down-to-earth. What a pity he's going back to England so soon. End of July, he said.'

'It's not a pity at all,' Melanie said sharply. 'You know I have no intention of marrying again. Don't start trying to matchmake me. You'll only be wasting your time. And don't go telling Royce what happened to Joel and David. He knows I'm a widow and that's all he's going to know. I'm not in the business of pity.'

Frieda put down the bean slicer, her face softening with just that emotion. Pity. 'You can't go on grieving forever, love. I thought... after last night... well, I hoped...'

'Well, you hoped wrong,' Melanie said, looping a stray lock of her hair back behind her ear and gnawing at her bottom lip.

The back wire-screen door opened at that vulnerable moment and in walked Royce, wearing a spiffy grey tracksuit and trendy black running shoes. Despite having dark rings under his eyes and sporting a five-o'clock shadow, he looked far too attractive to her eyes. A hot awareness of her nudity under the dressing-gown had her clutching the lapels tightly over her chest and battling an irritatingly embarrassed feeling. Silly, really, in the circumstances. There wasn't an inch of her he hadn't already seen. *And* from very close quarters!

Wayne blundered in after Royce, looking chirpier than he had the night before. 'Hi, Aunt Mel. Royce here fixed my bike. That's worth one of Dad's beers, don't you think?'

'Indubitably,' Melanie said, throwing Royce a dry look. He returned it with arrogant confidence, coming over to pull out a chair next to hers. Melanie resisted the temptation to flee to her bedroom, decided it just might do him good to see her in her ancient pink dressing-gown and bare feet. Till she remembered he'd found her madly attractive *before* she'd done herself up last night, when she'd been dreary Mrs Lloyd—housekeeper. Lord knew why.

'Hi, Mel,' he said, adopting Wayne's casual abbreviation of her name. 'How's the bod this morning? Stiff and sore, I'll bet.'

Melanie stared at him.

'From all that dancing,' he added, a wicked gleam in his eye.

'I used to love dancing,' Frieda said wistfully from behind her bean slicing. 'But Ron doesn't take me any more. I'm hard pushed to get him to take me to the club for a meal and a game on the pokies. He says you get beyond dancing.'

'Well, his sister's not beyond it,' Royce said. 'No, siree. Never been with a better mover in all my life.'

Melanie glared at him but he merely winked at her.

'Get that into you,' Wayne said, plonking a can of beer down in front of Royce, who popped the can and drank deeply.

'Ah,' he sighed afterwards. 'Never thought I'd like cold beer but it sure hits the spot after a bit of physical work.'

'Dad'll be pleased the bike's going at last. He wasn't too happy with me buying it and all, was he, Mum?'

'You can say that again. So tell us, Royce, what are you going to do when you get back to England? Wayne tells us you've retired from Formula One racing.'

'I have, indeed. Other than refurbishing a house I bought a while back, I've no definite plans. I might take up playing polo. I've always wanted to do that.'

'And what about your family?' Frieda persisted, much to Melanie's annoyance. 'Any brothers and sisters?'

'Nope. I was an only child. After my mother had me, she declared having babies her least favourite pastime, with being poor a close second. She left us that same year. I haven't seen her since, but I heard she was married to some rich aristocrat in London. Actually I never missed her at all, but Dad was pretty cut up about it for the rest of his life. Poor sod. Still, he's dead now . . .'

Though these words were delivered in a very casual fashion, Melanie could not help but hear the bitterness in Royce. Possibly this was the reason he'd never married, a thought Frieda must have had as well.

'And you never married yourself, Royce?' she asked. 'Melanie wasn't too sure if you ever had or not.'

'Really?' He slanted her a dry look. 'I thought you knew I was a confirmed bachelor.'

She shrugged. 'One can't always believe what one reads in the magazines and newspapers.'

'I'm so glad you think like that. Now I won't have to work so hard to convince you that all you've read about me isn't true.'

Her returning look was sardonic. 'I see no reason for you to convince me of anything.'

'Oh, dear,' Frieda piped up into the sudden, tense silence. 'I've just remembered, we've nearly run out of milk. Wayne, could you run me down to the shops. Melanie, you wouldn't mind if we used your car, would you?'

'I could take you,' Royce offered.

'Oh, no, you're a visitor. You stay and talk with Melanie. Even if she *isn't* dressed.' This last remark was delivered with a look which implied she was blowing her chances with this man, presenting herself in such a dishevelled state and being generally awkward.

Melanie handed over her car keys with some reluctance, not because she was afraid Wayne would wrap it around a pole, but because she didn't want to be alone with Royce. The banging of the back door, followed by the sound of her car being started up, signalled for her to extricate herself from the kitchen post-haste. She stood up, scraping back the chair as she resashed the old robe tight around her naked flesh.

'I'd love to stay and chat,' she said sarcastically. 'But I really must go and dress.'

'Not on my account,' he drawled, tipping up the can to finish his beer. 'I prefer you with as few clothes on as possible.'

Melanie counted to ten, all the while glaring at him. 'I'd ask why you're here, if I didn't already know.'

His hard blue gaze swept up her body to her flushed face. 'So why *am* I here? I'd really like to know what you're thinking. It could be interesting, being privy to that schizophrenic mind of yours. In fact, it might satisfy a little of my curiosity about what makes you tick, Melanie Lloyd.'

Her black eyes spat angry fire at him even as she laughed. But her anger and fire hid a dangerous excitement and arousal. Melanie's earlier resolve to go along with his charade for a while was swamped by an urgent need to get him out of this house and away from her. *Now*!

'Then you'll have to satisfy your curiosity without any help from me,' she flung at him. 'And you'll have to satisfy your *other* needs in future without any help from me as well. I'd have thought you'd have got the message when you woke to find me gone. I don't like postmortems to my one-night stands, or encores. So if you'll just toddle off back to your cave I'll find some excuse for your absence when Frieda and Wayne return.'

'No,' he said. Simply. Casually.

Everything inside Melanie began to disintegrate—her confidence plus her desire to resist what he so obviously wanted. Those sexy blue eyes told her everything as they locked with hers.

'I...I don't want you here, Royce,' she said, trying to sound very firm but failing abysmally. 'I didn't invite you. I want you gone. I...I don't want to see you again. Ever.'

'What an incorrigible liar you are, Melanie. First of all, you don't have one-night stands. Secondly, you don't want me gone at all, and you sure as hell want to see me again.' He got to his feet and walked slowly round to where she was standing at the end of the kitchen table. The steely resolve in his gaze both excited and frightened her. When his hands shot out to pull her hard against him, she panicked.

'No!' she cried, struggling in his arms so that his mouth could not find its target. 'Let me go!' She began to hit him everywhere, flailing arms connecting with his arms, his chest, his shoulders, his head.

She twisted and he pushed till her struggles were half defeated by the backs of her thighs digging into the edge of the kitchen table. His hard elbows pressed her arms down uselessly by her sides while strong hands captured the sides of her head, holding it still for his marauding mouth.

She could have bitten him, if she'd really wanted to. Could have still kicked him in the shins or brought her knee up into his groin. But Royce had been right, of course. She didn't want him gone at all. At least... her body didn't.

God, but she hated the way it sagged submissively beneath his, a moan escaping her mouth as her lips fell helplessly apart.

He needed no further invitation, using his considerable kissing skill to bend her further to his will, to bend her back on to the table and peel open her dressing-gown. She knew what she was allowing was shocking and decadent, but she couldn't seem to resist with his mouth all over her like that.

Till she dazedly remembered something...

'No, you can't,' she croaked, battling to lift her head a little.

But then his lips found the ultimate target and her head clunked back on to the table, her protest dying. Oh, God, he was good at that. So very, very good.

At least that was safe enough, she told herself weakly. And with a soft moan, gave herself up to the heady delights his lips and tongue were evoking.

Only it wasn't safe. For at a point when her head was whirling, and her body was shattering into a million pieces, things changed swiftly and smoothly to the real thing. By the time her befuddled brain could react to the difference, Royce was already pumping his seed into her body, into her unprotected, possibly fertile body.

'Oh, no,' she sobbed, struggling to sit up. 'No...'

Tears of despair and horror welled up in her eyes, flooding over. She scrambled back on to the table, sending fortunately empty beer cans flying, kicking him away from her, hating him. 'Go away. Get out. Get *out*!'

He stared at her, clearly stunned. 'Melanie, for God's sake! What's wrong? Why are you acting like this? You wanted it. You know you wanted it!'

He was hurriedly fixing his clothes when there was the sound of a car pulling into the driveway, the sound of doors opening and closing. Melanie's horror soared, stricken eyes flying to the back door.

Before she could do anything, Royce acted, sweeping her off the table and carrying her quickly down the hallway, eyes darting from side to side till he found the bathroom. He placed her down on unsteady feet, wrapping and sashing the robe tightly around her.

'I'll tell them you're showering,' he said, and went to leave. But then he glanced back at her standing there, crying, and groaned.

'Don't cry,' he said raggedly, and swept her back into a fierce embrace. 'There's no reason to cry, dammit! What is it? Are you worried because I didn't use anything? I told you before that I was no risk to your health and since you're on the Pill there's no harm done.'

Oh, God, he thought she was on the Pill. But she wasn't. She'd used a diaphragm last night, and it had been removed this morning when she'd woken up.

'You don't understand,' she sobbed against his chest.

'No. No, I don't understand. I don't understand you at all, Melanie.' He held her away from him with firm, steadying hands. 'And I'm not going to go away till I do.'

Her blurred eyes flew open but he was gone, striding back down the hall, his strong male voice floating back for her to hear. 'That didn't take you long, Frieda? Here, can I help you with that? Melanie's popped into the shower. She won't be long. So tell me, is there anything else I can do? Some veg to peel, perhaps?'

Frieda's laughter was coy. 'What kind of hostess would I be, making the visitors do the vegetables? No, you go out on to the back porch and have another beer with Wayne. I'll send Melanie out to join you when she's looking more presentable.'

Melanie shut the bathroom door and clasped anguished hands to her head. What was she going to do?

Maybe you'll be lucky, the voice of desperate hope suggested. Maybe you won't get pregnant. There's no need to panic yet. No need to do anything. Pull yourself together, girl. The last thing you want is Royce getting a whiff of what might have occurred just now. Men like him had a very possessive streak about things they thought they owned. Children they fathered came under that category. After that ball next month, he'll be safely on his way back to England. By then you should be sure one way or the other and, if the worst comes to the worst, you will have to take the appropriate steps.

A shudder ran through her right down to her toes. For she suspected she might not be able to do that, take an innocent child's life as Joel had taken an innocent child's life. But what was the alternative?

Snapping on the shower, she threw aside her dressing-gown and stepped under the icy shards of cold water. It beat down upon her body, stinging and harsh. I'm being punished, she thought. Punished.

But for what? What have I ever done that was so wicked? Have I deceived anyone, betrayed anyone, destroyed anyone? I was the victim in my marriage, not the villain. But I'm not going to be a victim again in any relationship, however fleeting it may be. Not now. Not ever!

By the time she stepped out of the shower, the new Melanie was back in control.

CHAPTER TEN

By the time Melanie emerged, dressed in washed-out jeans and a dark purple mohair jumper, her black hair caught back with a black velvet ribbon, her only make-up some burgundy lipstick, she was fully composed. Frieda waved her out of the kitchen, having always been possessive about her cooking, so Melanie had no option but to wander out on to the back porch where Wayne and Royce were stretched out in the watery winter sun, drinking another beer.

'You'll be over the driving limit if you don't watch it,' she warned drily, dragging up a deckchair and settling herself next to Royce, while doing her best to ignore his smoldering gaze. God, did he have to look at her that way, as if he was remembering what she looked like without any clothes on?

'It's light beer, Aunt Mel,' Wayne informed her. 'Only two per cent. He can have quite a few and still be fit to drive.'

Melanie laughed. 'I doubt Royce is ever fit to drive on normal roads. You should have seen him last night. We went careering up Parramatta Road like we were in the Indianapolis 500.'

'She's exaggerating,' Royce refuted. 'Your aunt's a bit of a nervous Nellie in a car.'

'Well, that's only to be expected, I suppose,' Wayne muttered, giving his aunt a sympathetic look. 'What with the car accident and all.'

'You were in a car accident, Melanie?' Royce asked, turning a disarmingly concerned face towards her.

'No, I—'

'Not Aunt Mel,' Wayne interrupted before she could shut him up, though she snapped forward on her chair and shot him a warning glare.

'Sorry, Aunt Mel,' he mumbled. 'I...I forgot you don't like to talk about it. Maybe I'd better make myself scarce.'

'Maybe you should,' she bit out, before relenting. 'Don't be silly, Wayne. There's no reason Royce shouldn't know. My husband was killed in a car accident. That's what he was going to say,' she finished firmly, hoping Wayne got the message that David was not to be mentioned.

'I see,' Royce said, eyeing her closely. 'I'm sorry. And I'm sorry for the way I drove last night. I didn't realise...'

'How could you?' she said nonchalantly, and leant back, her cool façade not betraying her twisted insides.

'I guess I couldn't since you didn't see fit to tell me,' he said with reproach in his voice. 'How long ago did this happen?'

'Four years.'

'Four years... and were you married long?'

'Eight years,' she admitted curtly.

'That's a long time to be married without any children,' he remarked.

'Yes, it is, isn't it?' she returned airily.

Wayne started coughing at this point and stood up, saying he was going to see if he could help his mother.

'A discreet retreat,' Royce murmured once the wire door banged shut. 'I like that boy.'

'He's hardly a boy,' she snapped. 'He's man enough to be sleeping with his girlfriend without truly caring for her, like most macho males. Luckily, she had enough common sense to give him the heave-ho.'

'Would you like me to give him some words of worldly advice?' Royce countered caustically. 'I could suggest he start sending the girl red roses and telling her he loves her every other day. Women go for that.'

'You've tried it, have you?' she asked tartly.

'No, but I've seen it work for other men.'

'You don't need such niceties, though, do you? You do extremely well on the "*veni, vidi, vici*" style of operations. "I came, I saw, I conquered". It must be great to be so goddamned irresistible!'

'Irresistible, am I? How flattering. I didn't realise. So tell me, darling Melanie,' he whispered, leaning close so that she could feel his warm breath on her cheek, 'have I conquered you?'

She was infuriated by the way her heart flipped over at his cynical endearment, not to mention his closeness. Her unwanted reactions sparked a bitter anger that found solace in fighting words.

'You've got to be joking, lover,' she spat at him. 'What happened last night was all *my* idea, not yours. I needed a man at long last, and I decided you would do better than most for reasons which should be obvious. You danced to *my* tune, Mr King-of-the-Road, not the other way around!'

His hand shot out to grab her chin, twisting it cruelly with steely fingers. 'And the episode just now on the kitchen table?' he derided. 'Who was dancing to whose tune then? I had you in the palm of my hand, lover. Literally. And I could have you again, any time I want.' He released her chin with a flick of his hands, his mouth curling.

'You wanna bet?' Her glittering black eyes locked with his, challenging him, despising him. 'Why don't you kiss me, Royce?' she hissed. 'Go on, I dare you to. Kiss me and feel my coldness. Kiss me, and feel my contempt. Kiss me, and feel my hatred for men like you!'

His head jerked back, blue eyes wide as he stared at her in horror and what might have been hurt, if he'd been capable of really being hurt. Merely a bruised ego, Melanie decided bitterly. Men like Royce didn't feel real pain.

'I see you're finally getting the message, Royce,' she resumed in the cool, remote voice she'd been comfortable with for years, but which had deserted her since meeting Royce. Thankfully, it was now back to save her. 'It's over. *We're* over. I do hope you will respect my wishes and not try to contact me again after today. If you do, I might have to complain to Byron that you're sexually harassing me. I doubt he would look kindly on that. Byron is rather a stickler when it comes to moral issues.'

Royce's stunned face gradually took on a stony mask, his eyes hardening to blue chips of ice. 'In that case, he wouldn't look kindly on his housekeeper whoring around with a man she'd just met!'

Melanie paled, and for a second time Royce actually looked stricken with a type of remorse. But then Wayne called through the screen door that dinner was ready, and any expression of apology melted away.

'Let's cool this for your family,' he muttered. 'There's no need to upset them, is there? This is just between us, after all.'

Melanie found dinner an awful strain. Royce carried off the charade of superficial politeness the better of the two. Over coffee, he actually pulled photos out of his wallet, showing the others snaps of the sixty-room mansion that awaited him back home. It was, indeed, magnificent. Almost a castle, set in huge grounds rather like a park.

'It's so big!' Frieda exclaimed. 'I wouldn't like to have to keep it clean, I can tell you.'

'Looks good to me,' her son joked. 'I could be as messy as I liked an no one would find out for six months. It'd take that long to get round all the rooms.'

Royce chuckled. 'It would if only one person had to do all the work. But I have an army of cleaners and gardeners who are getting everything into shape. I'm going to open it to the public during the summer months, then in the winter I'm going to hire out the grand dining-room and the ballroom for functions and parties. Hopefully, that will pay for the tax and upkeep, which is astronomical. It sent the lord who used to own it stony broke.'

'I suppose you bought it from this poor bankrupt aristocrat for a song,' Melanie said, unable to hide the hostility in her voice. Frieda shot her an amazed look which she steadfastly ignored.

'I did get it for a song,' Royce admitted drily. 'But the poor bankrupt aristocrat had actually passed on to that great polo field in the sky, and since he'd neither married, nor had any living relatives, the place was put

up for auction by the charity he'd left it to. Yours truly
made the winning bid.'

'Who are you going to leave it to when you go, Royce?'
Wayne asked innocently. 'You're not married either, and
don't have any children. Or do you?' he added with a
cheeky wink.

'Wayne!' his mother reprimanded.

Melanie found her hand automatically resting on her
stomach, butterflies crowding in as she thought of the
possible consequences to what had happened in the
kitchen earlier. What would she do if she were pregnant?
If she did decide to keep the baby, she would have to
quit her job and come back to live with Ron and Frieda.
She had no money except for her meagre savings from
her salary over the past two years, Joel having left her
nothing from their marriage. Their fancy furnished house
had been rented, and his small insurance payout had only
just covered the cost of the funerals and her medical
expenses afterwards. Even the car he'd driven had been
leased. They had owned nothing of any value except two
wardrobes full of very expensive clothes.

She was reefed back to the present by Royce's droll
answer.

'As far as I know, I have no offspring,' he was saying.
'And believe me, Wayne, if a man in my position fathers
a child, he doesn't get away with it these days. The lady
in question would have me in court quicker than you
could blink, with DNA tests and God knows what else
to prove her case. So I can safely say I have not added
to the population problem of this world. Now to answer
your original question, I dare say I too will end up leaving
my fortune to charity. Cancer research perhaps.'

'My mother died of cancer,' Frieda said sadly. 'It's a
dreadful disease.'

'Yes, it is.'

'Must we talk about such wretched topics?' Melanie
said, leaping up to start clearing the table. It was nearing
three and she wanted to steer Royce out of here before
her brother came home at four. She had just about had
enough worrying over what would be said next.

Royce must have been of a similar mind because he stood up also, and offered to help with the washing-up.

'No need for that,' Frieda smiled. 'Ron bought me a dishwasher for Christmas last year. Maybe you and Melanie might like to go for a drive?'

'What a good idea. What do you say, Mel? You were going to show me Darling Harbour today, remember?'

Her eyes met his, warning him that her agreeing was a white lie simply to get them out of the house. 'Yes, all right. But we'll have to drive both our cars into the city. It's too far for me to drive back here and then back to Belleview.'

'Fair enough. You can lead and I'll follow. That way you can't accuse me of driving recklessly.'

Melanie made no comment on that, merely said she had to collect some things from her room. Packing her housekeeping clothes in a plastic bag, she emerged looking collected, though her insides would continue to churn till she was safely away from Royce and back in Belleview.

'Ron's going to be annoyed that he missed you, Royce,' Frieda said as she walked with them out through the front gate and into the street. 'Maybe you'll be able to come back for dinner again some time soon.'

'I'm not sure I'll have another opportunity,' Royce returned. 'I'm flying to Melbourne in the morning.'

'But I thought you were staying in Sydney till late July!' Frieda protested, echoing Melanie's surprise.

'You must have misunderstood me,' he explained smoothly. 'I *will* be back in Sydney for a day or two around then to go to the auction, but meanwhile I'll be travelling around the rest of Australia.'

'What a shame! So this is goodbye, then?' she held out her hand.

He took it, giving her a warm smile. 'I'm afraid so, but it's been a grand day. I'll remember it always.'

Against all common sense Melanie felt tears pricking at her eyes. So this really was goodbye...

Gathering herself, she cleared her throat, thanked Frieda once more for the meal and strode over to her small, second-hand sedan. Royce slipped in behind the wheel of the Ferrari, the engine rumbling to life immediately. Mclanie belted up and started her engine, signalling carefully before she negotiated a slow U-turn and crawled down to the corner. A glance in the rear-view mirror showed the black sports car close to her bumper-bar, a wry expression on Royce's face.

Undeterred, she crawled out on to Parramatta Road where she proceeded sedately along in the slow lane. Royce was content to follow for a short distance till suddenly he zapped out from behind and drew alongside, gesturing for her to pull over in the next side-street. When she shook her head vigorously, he merely cut her off and forced her to turn or have a small collision.

She was shaking by the time she pulled up. But with what? Nerves? Anger? Fear? She was still standing there, quivering, when Royce jumped out of his car, slammed the door and stalked back with thunder on his face. Reefing open her door, he stood glaring down at her, hands on hips.

'Why couldn't you just damned well turn when I asked you? Or did you expect me to crawl after you at ten miles an hour all the way into the city?'

'I don't expect anything of you, Royce Grantham,' she bit out, a clenched jaw the only way she could stop her teeth from chattering.

'Fine! Because I'll like nothing better than to live down to your low expectations. I won't say it's been a pleasure knowing you, my dear. It's been sheer torture! With a bit of luck I'll find some nice normal lady in Melbourne who'll be so uncomplicated she might even prove boring. But I'm sure I can cope with some boredom after you. Hell, yes!'

He laughed and straightened, looking down at her coldly now. 'I won't kiss you goodbye. You might have painted your lips in some deadly poison like all black widows. One word of warning, though, before I go. Don't get into the habit of insulting your lovers after you've finished with them. You never know who or what they might be. I'd hate to wake up one morning and read about the beautiful housekeeper of Belleview found murdered in her bed!'

Whirling, he strode back to the Ferrari, climbing in without a backward glance. Gunning the engine, he scorched round in a sweeping curve and was gone, leaving nothing behind but the smell of tyres burning.

Unless one counted the shattered woman sitting, sobbing, in the front seat of a plain grey car. Or the child of his she was possibly carrying.

Gemma arrived at work on the Monday morning, feeling better than she had in ages. She'd made up with Nathan on the Saturday night as planned, they'd enjoyed a wonderful meal at home that she had cooked and, best of all, she'd had no need to pretend a thing later in bed. It had been marvellous, even if she remained as conservative in her lovemaking as ever. The icing on the cake had been that Nathan hadn't fallen straight to sleep afterwards, but held her in his arms, and actually talked to her about his writing.

Not much, mind. But a little, telling her that the play he'd been working on was not going according to plan—something to do with his characters not being able to find the right emotion—and that he was actually looking forward to directing the play Byron was producing, which was called *The Woman in Black*.

When she asked him what it was about, he declined to tell her, saying that he would prefer she knew nothing about it till she saw it on opening night. Which would be when? she asked. Months away, he told her. They hadn't even held auditions yet for the roles. But Lenore didn't have to audition, she slipped in. Why was that?

Gemma had been pleased by her husband's answer. It had nothing to do with him. Apparently, Byron had promised her the role some time back and refused to go back on his word. Nathan was not thrilled, but what could he do? He conceded Lenore probably would have been one of the favourites for the role, even if she *had* auditioned, because she was the right age and physical type for the part, and was one of Sydney's most experienced and professional stage actresses. Still, he would not tolerate any rumours of nepotism where she was concerned. If Lenore didn't come up to scratch she'd be out on her ear like a rocket. He had Byron's agreement on that.

Gemma had been soothed by Nathan's dismissive and dispassionate manner when talking about his ex-wife. He seemed to consider her presence in the play a mild irritation, but certainly not worth getting het up over. Gemma could hardly keep thinking he still harboured deep feelings for her, in the circumstances.

Oh, yes, Saturday had been a success all round, especially when it came to improving their communication. Gemma decided it had been worth the sacrifice to her pride not to make a fuss about Nathan's cavalier and chauvinistic behaviour that morning. Her patience had been rewarded by a happy evening, crowned by an even happier Sunday.

Kirsty, at long last, had telephoned her, and they had the loveliest long chat. Apparently Nathan had torn strips off his daughter the day before, castigating her for her immature and selfish attitude toward Gemma. After he'd left, she'd chatted with her mother and had finally seen the error of her ways. She'd been all apology and sweet forgiveness, so much so that Gemma had been touched beyond belief. She hadn't realised till then that Kirsty's withdrawal of her friendship had been like a huge shadow over her marriage to Nathan. Now, that shadow had lifted and she felt so happy that she couldn't stop smiling as she dusted the counter and waited for her first customer of the day.

Unfortunately, that first customer wiped the smile from her face.

'Mr Grantham!'

'Royce, please.'

Her eyes darted nervously towards the door, afraid all of a sudden that Nathan would come in and catch them together again. Crazy, since she knew he'd gone straight to Byron's office where they were going to discuss more arrangements for their production of *The Woman in Black*. Still, Whitmore's head office wasn't all that far away and it wouldn't take Nathan long to walk along here if he chose to for some reason.

'I . . . I can't talk to you,' she whispered agitatedly.

'Why not, for heaven's sake? Oh, I see. You're worried about your bully-boy of a husband seeing us together.'

'He is not a bully-boy,' she defended hotly. 'How dare you call him that? Why, he's . . . he's . . .'

'*Can* it, sweetie. I'm not in the mood this morning. I wouldn't have come in here at all except I was on my way to the airport and spied you in here and I just couldn't leave without having my curiosity satisfied about one thing. Was Melanie happy in her marriage or not? Or don't you know the answer?'

'I . . . I don't have any first-hand knowledge,' Gemma stammered, flustered by the whole scenario. 'I . . . I didn't know Melanie back then, before her husband and baby were killed, that is.'

'*What* did you say?'

'I said I didn't know her back then.'

'No, no, not that. The bit about her baby being killed. She had a *baby*? And it was killed in the same accident that her husband died in?'

'Yes, that's right. I was told it happened in front of her very eyes, down the street from her home. Apparently, she was devastated for ages and still hasn't really gotten over it. At least . . .' She had been going to add that she thought Melanie might have been on the road to recovery with her obvious attraction for *him*. But since he was leaving Sydney, there was no point in telling him that, was there?

'Good God,' he muttered.

It was then Gemma noticed how terrible he was looking. Bleary-eyed and unshaven, like he'd been out drinking all night.

'Poor bitch,' he added, shocking Gemma.

'You shouldn't talk about Melanie like that. It's . . . it's . . . disrespectful.'

'It's the bloody truth. Hell, I wish I'd known this sooner.'

'Why? Do you think you could have persuaded her to go out with you if you'd known more about her?'

Gemma was taken aback by the odd gaze he set upon her. Was he laughing behind those harsh, glittering blue eyes—or crying? Why did she suddenly feel so terribly sad looking into them?

'Royce,' she said gently, reaching out to touch him on the arm, 'if this means anything to you, I think she liked you, despite everything.'

'I doubt that, sweet child. I doubt that very much. Still, it's a nice thought to leave on. A very nice thought...'

'You won't be back for the ball, then?'

A haunted look joined the weary sadness. 'I'm not sure. Maybe, if I want to punish myself a little more. Will she go, do you think?'

'Melanie? No, I don't think so. She never goes out anywhere, except to her brother's for dinner every Sunday. She's a very sad, lonely lady. For... for what it's worth, I don't think she was very happily married.'

'What makes you say that?' he asked sharply.

Gemma shrugged. 'It's only a hunch, really. Sometimes, when Melanie talks about marriage and men, there's a certain bitterness in her voice that can't be explained by the accident. She doesn't talk about the past, but it's always there, I think, colouring everything she does and feels.'

'I can appreciate that,' he said ruefully. 'The past can have a way of poisoning the present. It's like a festering sore that needs to be cut out before it contaminates everything. Still, that's easier said than done, isn't it?' he finished drily. 'I suppose you'll be at the ball with your bodyguard hovering by your side?'

Gemma blushed at this description of Nathan. 'I...yes, I suppose.'

'Then I'll do you a favour and ignore you.'

He swung round then, and walked over to stare at the opal in the window. 'How much do you think it will take to secure this rock?'

'A million. Maybe a lot more if you've a serious rival for its possession.'

'That's a lot of money for something you can only look at...'

Whirling suddenly, he strode from the store without saying goodbye, without looking back. Gemma was left staring after him, an overwhelming feeling of depression descending to blot out her earlier happiness. What a shame nothing had come of his interest in Melanie. It was quite clear he'd been very taken with her. In Gemma's opinion, Melanie was a fool to turn her back on life, and such a nice man. No matter what Nathan said, no one would ever convince her that Royce Grantham wasn't a decent type, that his intentions hadn't been honourable. One only had to see the look in his eyes to see he was a very disappointed man.

Finally, she gave herself a mental shake and turned away to get on with her cleaning, but, try as she might, she couldn't recapture the same optimism about the day or the future that she'd woken with. Something Royce said kept coming back to bother her as well, something about the past being like a festering sore, spoiling things in the present. Once again, she started wishing Nathan could confide in her about *his* past, as well as let her explore her own more fully. The idea she'd once had about going back to Lightning Ridge to see what she could find out herself resurfaced.

And while it continued to tease her all day, she knew she would not mention it to Nathan that night, which underlined the continuing delicate nature of her relationship with her husband. Last Saturday night hadn't changed the *status quo* much after all, and this thought made her miserable. Suddenly, the future seemed intolerably grim, and she wanted to sit down and cry.

The arrival of a group of Japanese tourists put paid to that idea. Gemma sighed, dredged up a smile and walked over to them.

CHAPTER ELEVEN

'I'M SO excited!' Ava said, and put down her paint-brush. 'Only one more day to the ball. Do you really like my dress, Melanie?'

Melanie glanced round from her dusting and smiled at Ava. 'You've already asked me that a dozen times since I came into the room. Yes, I like your dress. It's lovely and you'll look lovely in it. Blue is definitely your colour.'

'It is, isn't it?' Ava jumped up, almost knocking the easel over. She grabbed it just in time, heaving a sigh of relief and throwing Melanie a sheepish look. 'I might have lost a few pounds lately but I still haven't lost my clumsiness.'

'Maybe not entirely,' Melanie agreed, 'but you've definitely improved. Do you realise you haven't broken anything in ages? And we all knock into things occasionally, you know.'

'I suppose so,' Ava smiled, then walked over to admire her dress once more.

What a sweet nature that woman has, Melanie was thinking as she watched her. She was so grateful to Byron for offering to take her to the ball, when in truth her big brother probably didn't have anyone else to take, and he'd be too proud to arrive at the Whitmore-sponsored Opal Ball unaccompanied.

Melanie sighed wearily at the cynicism of her thoughts. Maybe she was doing Byron a disservice. He had changed somewhat since the accident that had claimed his wife, actually developing a slightly more caring and considerate nature.

Still, he *was* a chauvinist, and a typical man. Men, she'd found, rarely appreciated a woman's way of looking at things. Men lacked sensitivity. They were also incredibly selfish and self-absorbed.

Such thinking sent her mind flying to Royce, and her heart twisted with a rueful anguish. She wouldn't mind betting he hadn't given her more than a passing thought since his departure from Sydney.

There again, why should he? Her behaviour had been as appalling as his had been. The weeks since his leaving had given her plenty of time to look back and try to understand how she had come across to him, how he would have perceived her as a woman.

And she didn't like the answers she'd come up with. Dear lord, he had every excuse to treat her as he had treated her. And to leave her in the manner he had. She'd deserved no better.

But she had suffered for her misdeeds and reckless foolishness. She was still suffering.

Her eyes dropped to her wristwatch. It was almost eleven. She'd promised to ring the doctor this morning and give him her final decision. She was booked into a small private clinic for the following Sunday evening and while she knew a termination was the most logical and practical solution to her problem—she tried to keep thinking about the baby growing within her as a *problem* and not a little person—there were moments of weakness and confusion when she just didn't know what to do.

Her doctor had counselled that he didn't think she was emotionally strong enough to have a baby alone after what had happened, that she would probably become an over-protective, exceedingly fearful mother who might eventually have another breakdown. The decision was up to her, of course, but it was clear what he was advising.

But he was a *man*, she worried anew. And an un-married, childless one at that. What did he know of being a mother? Melanie had known plenty of women over the years who'd been less than thrilled to find them-selves pregnant, but who, by the time the baby came, were besotted with their infant. Mother nature worked miracles with mothers, sometimes.

But maybe not with you, Melanie. What of the dreams just seeing a baby can evoke in you? No, not dreams. Nightmares!

Maybe the doctor was right. You can't take the risk. It wasn't fair to the child to have a permanently frightened mother.

The buzzing on the portable intercom in Melanie's pocket startled her, perhaps because it didn't buzz all that often. If people were expected at Belleview—visitors or tradesmen or the casual staff—then the gates were left open for them to simply drive in.

Drawing it from her pocket, she flicked the switch and spoke into the miniature microphone. 'Yes?'

'A delivery of flowers for a Mrs Melanie Lloyd.'

Ava swung round to stare at her. 'Flowers, Melanie? For you? Goodness, I wonder who they're from?'

Melanie's stomach did a somersault as the answer to Ava's question popped into her mind. Royce. It *had* to be Royce.

He'd said he was coming back for the ball. She'd thought he might change his mind and simply go straight back to England. But he hadn't. He'd come back to get his opal. And perhaps to say farewell to her in the only way he knew how.

A searing heat raced up her body and into her face, making a mockery of her recent decision never to sleep with any man ever again. The bitter realisation came that of course she had meant *other* men, not Royce. Nevertheless, it upset Melanie to think that, after all that had happened, she was still so susceptible to him. One would almost think that...

No, no, you fool, don't start thinking any such thing. What you feel is nothing more than it ever was. A strong physical attraction. A chemistry. A passion. Don't try to justify yourself any more by calling it love. You're a lot of things but never a hypocrite.

'I'll open the gates for you,' she told the waiting delivery man in cool, crisp tones. 'Go round to the side entrance near the garages.'

Melanie pressed the control that automatically opened the gates and hurried from the room, Ava bustling after her. 'Melanie?' she panted, breathing heavily in order to keep up. 'Who are the flowers from, do you know?'

Melanie saw no point in not telling the truth, especially with an avid Ava breathing down her neck. 'Yes, I think so. Royce Grantham.'

'But... but...'

'I'll explain later, Ava,' she said briskly. 'Right now I have to get to the side-door.' She increased her stride.

By the time Melanie reached the bottom of the marble staircase Ava had been left far behind. Despite her apparent composure upstairs, her pulse was racing madly by the time she reached the side-door. The sight of the delivery man holding a huge box with at least three dozen long-stemmed red roses resting under its transparent lid stopped her heartbeat for a second, before it lurched back into its pounding rhythm.

'Mrs Lloyd?' the delivery man checked, a slight frown on his face as he took in her drab appearance.

'Yes.'

He shrugged. 'Then these are definitely for you. You know, I usually only deliver this many roses to the maternity sections of hospitals. You have one very keen admirer here.'

Melanie took the roses, closed the door and leant against it, her fingers fumbling as she took the attached card out of its envelope. It simply said—'I've missed you, Royce.'

Missed me, have you? she thought angrily. You lying bastard! I know what you've missed. And I know what these roses represent. A ruthlessly cynical gesture, echoing your scathing remark that women fall for flower-giving and false avowals of love.

Tears pricked at her eyes as she realised how much she would give for him genuinely to have missed her, genuinely to have sent her these flowers out of true affection.

Oh, God... maybe I do love him.

No, you don't, argued back a darkly bitter voice. You're just thinking that because you've conceived his child, because you're trying to find an excuse to keep it. Grow up, Melanie. This is the real world and this is real life! So you have to make a tough decision here. Don't go all sentimental and wishy-washy on me. Do what has to be done!

Squaring her shoulders, she marched back along the corridor and into the kitchen where she would have dumped the roses in the garbage with the respect they deserved except that a breathlessly curious Ava was waiting for her there, ready to pounce.

'Oh, my goodness, I've never seen so many red roses! Oh, how beautiful they are. But horribly expensive. And were they from Royce Grantham?'

'Yes,' Melanie admitted curtly, which brought a sharp glance from Ava.

'You don't sound all that pleased, Melanie. Most women would be over the moon.'

'Naturally. That's what he's bargaining on.'

Now Ava was frowning. 'I don't understand. Actually, I don't understand any of this. I didn't know you even *knew* Royce Grantham in a personal way. Have you been seeing him since he came to dinner here that night?'

Melanie prayed for patience, and an inventive mind. 'Not the way you mean. I did go out with him once back then. But only once. He left Sydney several weeks ago and I haven't seen him since. I think he's come back for the ball and the auction of the Heart of Fire, and probably wants me to go with him. Celebrities don't like showing up in public without a partner. Don't make too much of the flowers, Ava,' she went on drily. 'Royce is a very wealthy man. He likes to impress ladies with grand gestures, that's all. It means little.'

'Are you sure? I mean, he must like you a lot, Melanie, to send so *many* roses. Goodness, I'm quite shocked, do you know that? I didn't realise you went out with men at all. I thought ... well, I thought ...'

'You thought correctly, Ava. I don't go out with men as a rule. This was a one-off thing. He was a stranger to Sydney and simply wanted someone to show him around one weekend. I did it as a favour,' she lied valiantly. 'As far as I know he flies out for England the day after the ball, so don't start making more of this than there is. It's a friendship of convenience at best, certainly not a romance.'

'Oh, what a pity! He was such an interesting and clever man. Just the sort who would have suited you, Melanie.'

Melanie laughed. 'You are an incorrigible romantic, Ava.'

'Perhaps. But what's wrong with that? This world could do with more romance, I say.'

'Yes, I'm sure it could,' Melanie agreed ruefully.

'You...you should think about getting married again, Melanie,' Ava continued gently. 'I know what happened to you was tragic but life does go on and you're a beautiful woman, no matter how hard you try to hide it. You shouldn't waste the rest of your life looking after Byron and me in this mausoleum. You should be looking after your own home, with a husband of your own, and children. Oh, yes, you should have more children. Do you think your poor little boy would want you to grieve for him forever? You'd make a wonderful mother. You...oh, no, what have I done? Oh, Melanie, I'm so sorry. I shouldn't have said anything. I...I...oh, please don't cry, Melanie. I'll go away. Yes, I'll go away right now and I'll shut my stupid mouth and I won't say another word on the matter ever again!'

'No, don't go!' Melanie cried, her whole being awash with floods of emotion. 'I...I'm not angry with you. It's just that...oh, just hold me, Ava. I really need someone to just hold me.'

Ava could do nothing to stop tears of heartfelt sympathy and remorse from rushing into her own eyes. Dear lord, she had never seen such misery, such emotional torture as was reflected at that moment in Melanie's eyes. And *she* had caused it, stupid fool that she was.

Clasping the weeping woman close to her not inconsiderable bosom, she hugged her and soothed her with halting and probably ineffectual words. 'I'm so...sorry.

It's none of my business . . . what you do. And who am I to talk? Miss Coward herself . . . staying at home all the time . . . hiding from life . . . pigging out on junk food . . . pretending . . . fantasising . . .'

Soon, it was Ava crying the harder of the two and Melanie doing the soothing. 'No, you were right to give me a talking to,' she reassured, reaching for a handful of tissues from the box on the counter behind them and sharing them out. 'But you're wrong about yourself. You're still relatively young, Ava, with most of your life left ahead of you. Do something with it before it is too late.'

Ava sniffled, dabbing at her eyes with the tissues. 'You really think I could?'

'Yes, I do. Get out of this house more often. Get a job of some sort, or volunteer for some charity work. Join a club. Anything! Only don't bury yourself in your room all the time. You can't make your dreams come true if you never give them a chance . . .'

'That's what Jade's always telling me. She gave me her mother's jewellery, did you know? Told me to sell it and use the money to go to proper art school, or go on a world cruise.'

'What a clever girl she is. Proper art school. Now why didn't I think of that?'

Ava sighed. 'Perhaps because I don't have any real talent in that department.'

'Ava! How can you say that? You *know* you have talent.'

'Byron doesn't think so,' she muttered.

'Well, pooh to Byron!'

Ava looked shocked. 'Pooh to Byron?'

'Yes, pooh!'

Ava started to giggle. 'I like that. Pooh to Byron.' Her giggles became real laughter. 'Pooh to Byron! I'll remember that the next time Byron tells me I'm stupid or I can't do something.'

'That's the spirit!'

'And you're going to look around for a nice man to marry,' Ava insisted in return.

Melanie smiled a wry smile. 'I can't promise miracles, but I'll certainly make some changes and decisions. And I'll stop running away from life too.'

'What a pity Mr Grantham is going back to England. He might have been your new Mr Right.'

Melanie's heart contracted. 'I think not, Ava. He's not the marrying kind.'

'No, I suppose not. Well, we're a right pair, aren't we? Blubbering on each other's shoulders and generally being silly-billies.'

'We all need a good cry occasionally.'

'I'm sure you're right, but I think I'd better go upstairs and wash my face. Some people can cry and still look gorgeous with big luminescent eyes but others we shall not name go all blotchy and puffy.'

Melanie laughed. 'Oh, go on with you.'

'I am going. In fact, I'm gone!' She waved airily over her shoulder as she hurried from the kitchen.

Melanie turned to look at the roses again. Ava was a dear but she just didn't understand. One couldn't always do what one might want to do down deep in one's heart. Sometimes, one had to be sensible...

Her hand was actually reaching up for the telephone to call her doctor when it rang. For a second, Melanie stared at it, intuition telling her, as it had with the flowers, who it was on the other end of the line. Feeling like a hunted animal, she suddenly wanted to run and hide, but what would be the good of that with a man like Royce? If she refused to talk to him on the telephone, he'd simply show up on her doorstep. Best to see what he wanted this time. As if she didn't already know.

Steeling herself, she lifted the receiver out of its cradle on the wall and placed it to her ear and mouth.

'Belleview,' she said crisply. 'Melanie Lloyd speaking.'

Royce's wry chuckle came down the line. 'Oh, yes, indubitably that is Melanie Lloyd. Who else could make me feel like a chastened schoolboy so quickly?'

'Royce,' she said in a flat, resigned tone.

'You remembered me? Or is it that my roses have arrived?'

Melanie swallowed the lump gathering in her throat. Why, after all these weeks, could the mere sound of his voice do this to her? Her heart hardened at her own stupidity.

'Yes, your roses have arrived,' she admitted in clipped tones. 'Am I to expect an imminent avowal of undying love as well? Or are you bargaining on our little separation having whetted my widow's appetite further for male company?'

His weary sigh made her feel guilty, her guilt alternately making her feel even angrier. 'What do you want, Royce?' she snapped. 'We said our goodbyes when you were last in town. Maybe I didn't make mine clear enough. Goodbye. I don't want to see you again.'

'Don't hang up on me!' he blurted out. 'Please, Melanie, don't hang up on me,' he repeated in a voice that stunned her. It was almost pleading, and highly emotional. It was not what she would ever have expected from Royce Grantham.

She didn't hang up.

'I'm sorry,' he said simply. 'For everything.'

It threw her. 'You...you behaved no worse than I did,' she found herself saying.

'I don't think so. I was the instigator of everything. I pursued you mercilessly, took advantage of you, exploited your vulnerability. Maybe I didn't realise quite why you were so vulnerable, but I was deliberately blind to your feelings, simply because I wanted you so much myself. I was selfish and arrogant and I'm deeply, deeply sorry if I hurt you.'

He sounded so sincere, as though she really meant something to him and he really cared. Melanie's heart leapt and, against all common sense, a vain hope sprang to life.

'Come to the ball with me tomorrow night,' he invited softly. 'I have tickets for two.'

She automatically cringed away from the Whitmores' seeing her at the ball with Royce.

'Melanie?'

She bit her lips and dithered.

'Don't you have anything to wear, is that it?'

'No, I have plenty of ballgowns I could wear over at my brother's place. My marriage was a very social one,' she finished with acid remembrance.

'I don't want you wearing any of those,' he said brusquely. 'I'll buy you something new and have it sent over.'

'Don't be silly, Royce. I might not like it and it probably won't fit.'

'If you like it and it fits, promise me you'll wear it.'

'You're being silly.'

'I'm being a man. *Promise* me.'

'All right, I promise. But only if I like it and only if it fits.'

'Fair enough. I'll have it to you by noon tomorrow. Is that in enough time?'

'Yes.'

'And I'll pick you up at your brother's place at eight again.'

'I . . . I don't recall agreeing to go with you to the ball in the first place. I think I've just been conned.'

'Would I con you?'

Yes, you would, she accepted bitterly.

Especially if the end result was to have her in his bed once more. God, Melanie, one phone call after all this time, for no other reason than he happened to be in town again, and you're hoping stupid hopes and agreeing to see him again. If he missed you so much and cared about you so deeply, where has he been for five weeks? He doesn't want anything different from what he did the last time. He's simply come up with a different approach this time to succeed and he just has.

'Are you still flying home to England the day after the ball?' she asked.

His hesitation to answer was very telling.

'That depends,' he said at last.

'On what?'

'I'll tell you tomorrow night at the ball.'

Melanie sighed. This is your chance to tell him that there isn't going to be a tomorrow night. So why aren't you saying something?

She did. 'All right.'

'Melanie . . .'

'Yes?'

'Thank you.'

'For what?'

'For saying yes. You won't regret it.'

But I already do, she sighed wearily as she hung up. Nothing had changed. Royce still didn't want marriage or forever. He wasn't in love with her. And he *had* just conned her.

So why had she agreed to see him one last time?

Perhaps because she knew that was what it was. One last time. One last night to remember, forever. A proper farewell for the father of her child.

Melanie sighed again, knowing at last what she was going to do. Picking up the telephone again, she checked the number of her gynaecologist and dialled. The receptionist answered and in due course she was put through to Dr Hyland.

'Melanie Lloyd here, Dr Hyland. Thank you for all your advice, but I ... I've decided to keep my baby.'

CHAPTER TWELVE

'ARE you sure this neckline isn't too low, Nathan?' Gemma asked, coming out of the bathroom with a frown on her face.

Nathan had commissioned the gown to be specially made for her, having found the style in a period costume book of Regency England. He'd said it was just the thing for her to wear to the ball, and Gemma had complied because her own sense of fashion was still a little unformed and she did like to dress to please her husband. Made of cream chiffon and lace, the high-waisted flowing style had looked all demure innocence in the book, but the wide square neckline had turned out to be more revealing than she'd realised, especially with her new underwear.

'I . . . I thought it was all right when I last tried it on, but that corset thing you bought me pushes my breasts right up and together, and with my hair up, I . . . I feel almost naked.' She placed a modest hand over her cleavage and smiled nervously at him. Frankly, the neckline wasn't all *that* low, but Nathan's previous displays of jealous possessiveness had made her careful over doing anything to encourage any untoward attention from other males. 'If you like, I could change.'

Nathan, who was looking impossibly handsome in a black formal dinner suit with white ruffled dress shirt and black bowtie, stared at her for several seconds before walking slowly around the foot of their king-sized bed, his eyes never leaving her. Picking up the covering hand, he lifted it to his mouth and kissed it. 'Don't be silly. You look delicious. Every man there tonight will be envious of me. The neckline is a little bare, but I've something for you to wear tonight that might help solve the problem.'

'Nathan, you haven't bought me more jewellery, have you?'

His head lifted, a frown settling into his beautiful grey eyes. 'You object to my giving you jewellery?'

'No, of course not, but you've given me so many presents since we've been married. Not a week goes by without you coming home with something.'

'Most women would be delighted,' he said stiffly.

'And so am I. Truly. But what are you going to do when Christmas comes? Or my birthday? They won't seem special if you give me things every other day.'

A wry smile pulled at his sensuous mouth. 'What a treasure you are, my darling. Not only sweetly innocent and delightfully modest, but totally without greed. Maybe that's why I like giving you things, because you don't ask for or expect anything.' Still smiling, he bent to kiss her lightly on the lips. 'You are a pearl beyond price. Which reminds me. Come over here...'

He drew her over to her dressing-table which was so full of his previous presents—other jewellery in a magnificent jewel box; bottles of perfume; cosmetics; delicate porcelain figurines; even a silver-handled brush and mirror set—that she wondered how he had found room for this new dark blue velvet jewel case.

'Open it,' he ordered.

She obeyed, her heart turning over at the sight of the triple pearl and gold necklace and matching drop earrings. If they were real pearls—and of course they were—they would have cost a small fortune. Gemma tried to feel happy, but her gasp and smile of pleasure felt false.

Over the past few weeks, the pattern of their marriage had changed. And so had Nathan.

He no longer burst forth from his study when she came home from work, eager to spend the entire evening with her, mostly because he himself was rarely home when she got in. He was still out holding auditions for his play—which was proving difficult to cast—or discussing sets with the set designer, or costumes with the costume designer, or whatever else a director did.

Invariably, when he came home he was tired and preoccupied, not wanting to go out so much. Not wanting to make love so much either. In fact he hadn't touched her this past week, which was beginning to bother Gemma a little. Her niggling concern that he would one day grow bored with her in that department was never far from her mind.

But one thing remained the same. She still felt like a highly prized possession, not a real wife, unless one thought of a wife as a totally submissive little thing who only opened her mouth to say, 'yes, sir, no, sir, three bags full, sir'. Nathan still made all their decisions without consulting her. Where they went, what they did, whom they invited over. The one time she'd been asked out by some of the girls at work for a girls-only night out, he'd made such a fuss—ranting and raving about the dangers of women being out at night without men to protect them—that she hadn't gone in the end.

'I thought pearls were just the thing for this dress,' Nathan was saying as he did up the clasp on the necklace, which had proven to be a choker and no real cover for her cleavage at all. 'Now that you're keeping out of the sun, your skin has lightened to a gorgeous honey colour.'

He trailed his fingers over her skin, then bent to press moist lips to the area of bare shoulder between the necklace and the beginning of the softly draped sleeves. Gemma shivered, but not, as she usually did, from pleasure. There was something odd about Nathan tonight, something dark and pensive that she didn't like. He seemed distracted, yet watchful. Every time he looked at her she had the feeling he was trying to see something. But what?

She suppressed an urge to sigh. Would she never get to know what he was thinking? Never find out what brought about the strange changes of mood that sometimes afflicted him? They'd be going along quite happily together when suddenly—was it something she did or said?—he'd become silent and almost morose, often giving her the blackest, most suspicious look. When that happened, she was at a loss what to do, as she was at a loss tonight.

She glanced in the mirror at Nathan standing behind her shoulder, and he was once again staring at her with that peculiarly intense expression in his eyes. Without stopping to think, she spoke her frustration aloud. 'Why do you keep on looking at me that way tonight, Nathan? You've been doing it ever since you came home.'

Immediately, his face was wiped of all expression and she could have screamed. As always when she dared to question him, he slotted that smooth mask into place, hiding everything from her. 'And what way is that, darling? You must know that I've always had trouble keeping my eyes off you. Especially in a dress like that.'

Their eyes met in the mirror, Gemma's angry with him for sidestepping her question. 'You were looking at me oddly long before I put this dress on, Nathan, and you know it. Why can't you just give me a straight answer for once? Every time I ask you a question you try to distract me with sweet talk so that you don't have to answer me.'

'What rubbish! I do no such thing. You women always imagine things. So I've been looking at you tonight. So what? You're my wife, aren't you? If you want me to be bluntly honest, Gemma, I've been wanting to make love to you from the moment I walked in the door, but you were busy getting ready for the ball, so I did the right thing and left you alone. I'm sorry if my *eyes* couldn't be similarly gallant,' he ground out, and, spinning away, strode angrily from the room.

Gemma stared after him, knowing in her heart that he was lying. She knew exactly the way he looked at her when he desired her, and that was not how he'd been looking at her tonight. The fact that he felt he had to lie over such a thing brought a rush of suspicions.

Was it that he couldn't bring himself to tell her that she was beginning to bore him? Had he perhaps met with Lenore today, and spending time with his beautiful ex-wife had made him see what a fool he'd been to marry a naïve child by comparison?

Gemma grabbed on to this last sickening suspicion, and ran with it. Maybe Nathan had not only seen Lenore today but lots of other days. Maybe the reason he hadn't been making love to *her* lately was because he didn't need to. Maybe he...

Gemma brought herself up with a jolt. This was all sheer speculation, the imaginings of a young and insecure bride. Still... it would put her mind at rest if Nathan would tell her where he'd been today, whom he'd been with. Surely she had a right to know that. Steeling herself, Gemma went in search of her husband.

She found him in his study, sitting at his desk and reading what looked like a report. Clearly, her sudden appearance in the doorway surprised him, for he jumped slightly in his chair.

'Good God, Gemma, you startled me. What do you want? Are you ready to go?'

'What are you reading?' she asked, more to see if she could get a straight answer for once instead of real curiosity.

'Nothing important. Just a quarterly report from one of my investment consultants.' He folded the sheets of paper, replaced them in a large brown paper envelope which he slipped into the top desk drawer. 'They're trying to get me to put some of my money back into the stock market.' His gaze raked over her. 'I see you haven't put your earrings in yet so you can't be ready. Surely you haven't come along here to keep on about my looking at you, have you?'

Gemma swallowed. 'No,' she lied. 'But I...I want you to tell me something, Nathan, please...just tell me the truth.'

His grey eyes cooled at this implication that he might not always tell her the truth. 'What is it?'

'I want to know where you went today. What you did. Whom you saw.'

'What is this, Gemma? What have I done to deserve the third degree?'

Panic at his continuing evasion stretched her nerves to breaking point. 'Once again you're going to side-step my questions, aren't you? Why can't you just tell me your movements, like any normal husband? What have you got to hide, for pity's sake?'

'Hide, Gemma? I'm not trying to hide a thing.' He got slowly to his feet, buttoning up his dinner-jacket as he made his way around the large desk. 'Look, I know I've been a bit distracted lately. This directing business is proving to be more time-consuming and involving than I realised.'

His handsome face melted into a disarming smile as he came up to her, curling gentle hands over her shoulders. 'As for telling you what I did today...I didn't realise you'd find it interesting. But if you must know we held more auditions for the part of the man opposite Lenore, and I'm glad to report we've at last found someone who might be able to carry off the demanding role.'

'*We*, Nathan?' Gemma pounced. 'Are you saying Lenore is always with you during these auditions?'

His smile faded, his eyes carrying total exasperation. 'Don't tell me you're still worried about Lenore. Good God, of *course* Lenore is present at the auditions! She does the reading with them. I have to see how they look and sound together. They have to spark off each other. Dammit, Gemma, if anyone has reason to be jealous in this marriage it's me! You've always got other men lusting after you.'

'That's not true!' she protested, her face flushing with frustration and fury.

'You don't see what happens behind your back, my dear,' he responded with dry sarcasm.

'If it does, then it's certainly not my fault,' she snapped. '*I* don't encourage them.'

'I know. That's why I do my best to protect you.'

'Then why let me wear this dress tonight?' she flung at him. 'Aren't you taking a risk, letting me show off my lust-inspiring body? Not that it seems to be inspiring much lust in *you* lately!'

When she went to whirl away he grabbed her, spinning her back hard against him, his fingers biting cruelly into her upper arm. 'You little cat, don't flex your claws with me or you might find yourself suddenly out of your depth.'

He grabbed both her arms and dragged her upward till their eyes were level. And their mouths. 'I've a good mind to rip that bloody dress off you right here and now and give you a taste of *real* lust. Then you wouldn't be so ready to be so damned nice to some of the men who flirt with you. You might also appreciate what it is I've been trying to protect you from!'

Gemma's eyes had rounded, her mouth falling open in utter shock. This was a Nathan she had never seen before. And he terrified the life out of her.

Did he see the terror in her eyes? Was that why he suddenly set her back down and released her arms, stepping back with a small shudder.

'I'm sorry if I frightened you,' he muttered. 'Not that you didn't deserve a shaking-up, Gemma. You're still incredibly naïve. But I shouldn't have lost my temper and threatened you like that. It won't happen again. Go and put your earrings on,' he ordered brusquely. 'We have to leave for the ball, or we'll be late.'

Nathan watched her stumble from the room, his face tight as a drum. Once she was gone he consciously relaxed his clenched fists and turned to go over to his desk where he pulled open the top drawer and stared down at the brown envelope.

The investigation into Gemma's past had cost him a small fortune, but the man Zachary had recommended had come through with the truth at last, complete with documentation. Unfortunately, the truth was so appalling that he had made the difficult decision to keep Gemma's past a secret, especially from her.

Difficult decision?

His mouth pulled back into a darkly rueful smile. It hadn't been all that difficult, had it, Nathan?

Shutting the drawer, he locked and removed the key, slipping it in his pocket. Smoothing the grimace of self-disgust from his face, he walked from the room.

* * *

'Oh, Melanie, you look lovely!' Frieda exclaimed. 'That dress fits you like a glove.'

'It does, doesn't it?' she said, still surprised. One would have thought it had been made for her, not bought off the peg.

She twisted to examine the dress in the mirror from all angles. The colour was deep purple, the material satin, the style sleek and sophisticated with a tightly fitted elongated bodice that swished out into a long flowing skirt. It had long tight sleeves and a low off-the-shoulder neckline that showed off her pale creamy skin to perfection, not to mention her bust.

Included in the dress box that had been delivered to Belleview by express courier at eleven that morning had been a black satin evening bag, black satin pumps—which also fitted perfectly—and a black satin ribbon choker to wear around her neck, a gold heart centring it.

Melanie had loved everything on sight but she was still amazed at the superb fit. 'I'd love to know how Royce...' Suddenly, the penny dropped and she whirled round. 'It was you, wasn't it?' she accused her sister-in-law. 'You gave Royce some of my clothes. And a pair of my shoes!'

Frieda didn't look at all shamefaced. 'Well, of course I did! The man's mad about you, Melanie. And I think you're mad about him. I'd have done anything he asked me to if it meant getting you two happily together again.'

Melanie shook her head in exasperation. 'You're almost as bad as Ava. Don't you know the sort of man Royce is? He's an adventurer where women are concerned. A regular Don Juan. He's been travelling around the world, no doubt bedding some woman in every city he visited. I was simply his Sydney woman.'

Frieda was taken aback by Melanie's startling admission. 'You *were*? You mean, you and he...'

Melanie said nothing.

'I suppose I shouldn't be surprised,' Frieda muttered. 'You're so beautiful...'

'And he's a highly skilled seducer of beautiful women,' Melanie inserted drily. 'So please, Frieda, let's have no more of talk of Royce being mad about me. Royce is not mad about me, except in as far as I can give him what he wants till he sets forth for home.'

Frieda flushed a bright pink, her face shocked. 'And you're still going to go to this ball with him?'

Melanie patted her hand gently. 'Don't worry about me, Frieda. I know what I'm doing.' In a fashion, she added silently and with a pang of real doubt. Presenting herself in public at this ball as Royce Grantham's partner might damage her in the eyes of her employer. Byron Whitmore would correctly conclude that Melanie had become Royce's lover during his stay in Sydney, and she had a feeling he wouldn't like that.

'But are you going to let him?' Frieda asked with round-eyed wonder. 'I mean . . . you know . . .' Her pink face became bright red.

'I . . . I'm not sure,' Melanie hedged, not wanting to shock Frieda too much. For she had thought of nothing else all day but being in Royce's arms again.

'Well, if you do,' Frieda whispered, 'don't forget to be careful. You don't want to be getting pregnant, do you?'

Melanie didn't know how she kept a straight face. 'I'll be very careful,' she returned, her lips twitching with the irony of it all.

'I think it's just as well Ron's having his Friday night drink with his mates,' his wife said, 'so that we don't have to explain any of this to him.'

'I couldn't agree more,' Melanie said, turning to give her hair a final brush and spray, then applying a liberal amount of Arpège perfume. 'Where's Wayne, by the way?'

'Over at his girlfriend's place.'

'Oh? Took him back, then, did she?'

'Yes, today. But you've got no idea what that boy did. Spent a fortune on sending her flowers. Long-stemmed red roses, would you believe? But it did the trick. She was on the telephone immediately, cooing like a dove.

Silly twit of a girl! Still, I shouldn't complain. I'm fed up with having that boy underfoot all the time. You've no idea how noisy and messy he is. Betty's mother's welcome to him! Oh, my, there's the doorbell. That'll be Royce. After what you've just told me I hope I can keep a civil tongue in my head. And let's hope he's come in something different from that sports car he was driving last time. Your lovely dress will crush if you have to squash yourself into one of those.'

He'd come in a white stretch limousine with grey velvet interior. And Frieda not only kept a civil tongue in her head, she fairly gushed all over Royce, who switched on the charm full-blast from the moment she opened the door. But he did look splendid in a black dinner-jacket with satin lapels and cummerbund which complemented Melanie's gown to perfection.

Melanie felt her stomach flip over at first sight of him, but it was his reaction to *her* that rattled her. Why did he stare so? Why look at her as though he'd never seen her before, or didn't know she could scrub up so well?

They didn't dilly-dally, and before long Melanie was settled in the spacious interior of the chauffeur-driven limousine and they were on their way towards the city.

'A glass of champagne for the lady?' Royce asked suavely, indicating the built-in bar.

'Why not?' She shrugged, and watched him fill the delicate flutes without spilling a drop. He handed her one glass and raised his in a toast. 'To the most beautiful woman in the world.'

'We're toasting Elizabeth Taylor?' she said drily.

'Please. I'm British. Though I *was* thinking of a certain dark-eyed, dark-haired beauty. Her name, however, is definitely not Elizabeth.' He clicked her glass and drank, his eyes never leaving hers.

Melanie had to admire his style. If she hadn't had some experience of Casanovas and con-men, she might have really been taken in by Royce. Still, that didn't stop the pain she felt when he worked his superficial charms upon her to such good effect.

In danger of succumbing to a sudden depression, Melanie lifted the glass to her lips and drank deeply. She'd promised herself not to become maudlin tonight. She'd accepted what he was and wanted their last night together to be a happy, carefree one. She took another swallow of the champagne.

'I know about the baby,' Royce said so unexpectedly that if there had been more champagne in her glass Melanie would have spilt it all over her dress. As it was, her hand shook terribly as she took the glass from her lips to stare at him in stark horror.

Seeing the glass tipping dangerously to one side, Royce swept it from her hands and put it back in the safety rack, along with his own. Melanie's trembling hands came to rest on her stomach, perhaps in an automatic and instinctively defensive gesture.

'You...you couldn't,' she rasped. 'I...I didn't t...tell...'

'Yes, I know, but I asked Gemma.'

'Gemma?' she repeated blankly.

He frowned. 'Yes. Gemma. Mrs Whitmore. The one who works in the opal store at the Regency. I dropped in there on my way to the airport on the Monday morning after we parted, driven to find out something about your marriage. She told me that it wasn't just your husband who was killed in that car accident, but a baby as well.'

Melanie shuddered with a type of perverse relief when she realised what baby Royce had meant. Then she shuddered again.

'I can't tell you how sad I felt for you,' he said softly. 'And how guilty. As I said on the telephone yesterday, I knew there had to be things in your past that made you act the way you were acting, but I didn't want to know in the beginning. I wanted you in my bed and I was prepared to turn a blind eye to your pain to achieve that end.'

Still in shock, Melanie just nodded, unable to say a word.

He picked up her closest hand and started gently stroking her fingers. 'I haven't been able to get you out of my mind, Melanie. I've tried. Dear God, I've tried, but I couldn't. I had to come back, had to find out if what I was feeling was more than I've ever felt before. And now I know. I think I love you, Melanie. I think I've loved you all along.'

Melanie's heart squeezed so tight that she thought it had to break. The roses had been bad enough, but did he have to follow them up with this? God, didn't he know it wasn't necessary? She'd already decided to go to bed with him again. A cold fury descended to rescue her from imminent disintegration, encircling her heart within an icy shell, holding it together, holding *herself* together.

'Is this what you told Wayne to tell his girlfriend?' she mocked. 'Don't look so puzzled, Royce. You did tell Wayne about the red roses strategy when you picked up my clothes from Frieda yesterday, didn't you?'

He was frowning at her. 'Surely you aren't angry with me for borrowing some of your clothes, Melanie, or for giving the poor boy a bit of advice? He looked so down-in-the-mouth. I couldn't let a fellow male suffer so I gave him a few clues. Did they work, do you know?'

'Oh, they worked. There again...they always work, don't they? I'm here, aren't I?'

'Melanie, for pity's sake, you don't think...' He groaned. 'God, what a bloody fool I am! I thought...I just wanted to... God-damn it, woman, I simply wanted to show you that you were different from any of my previous women. I never send flowers. Never!'

'You've never had to before,' she reminded him caustically.

He stared at her. 'What did that bastard of a husband do to you to make you like this? Don't deny it. I know he made you miserable. Gemma told me that...'

Her brittle laughter cut him off. 'Gemma? What would Gemma know of my marriage? Nothing! And that's exactly what *you're* going to know. My past is mine alone, and I don't appreciate people poking and probing into it, *or* talking about me behind my back. Accept victory gracefully, Royce. You've got what you wanted.

I'm going to the ball with you. Though frankly, I only agreed to come tonight because you were going home to England tomorrow and I felt badly about how we separated the last time. I like you. I really like you. You can be a sweet charming man, and you're an incredible lover. But don't insult my intelligence by talking of love. You don't love me. You don't even *know* me.'

'I'd damned well *like* to know you, but you won't give me the chance!'

'No, I won't.'

'Why?'

Why? She stared at him, steadfastly ignoring the confusion in her heart that he was talking like this, and grasping instead the certainty in her mind. Royce was another Joel. She'd sensed that the very first day they'd met, and she still sensed it. He'd come back to Sydney, not because he loved her, but to buy that damned opal. Royce did not really love her. No way. And she was never going to become involved with another man who didn't really love her.

'*Because*,' she said firmly.

'That's no answer.'

'It's the only one you're going to get.'

He shook his head, sighing in weary exasperation. 'I don't understand you. I don't think you understand yourself. Still, who am I to reason why?' he went on bitterly. 'My job is to pour champagne, be charming and an incredible lover, then get the hell out of your life in the morning. Simple. I've been doing that with women for years. I can do it on remote control. Would you like a little pre-ball sampler to show you what a good time you're in for tonight?' Abruptly, he pulled her into his arms.

'Royce, don't!' she cried, placing both hands on the hard wall of his chest and pushing at him quite ineffectually.

'Don't?' he scorned, his eyes contemptuous as he stared down at her trembling mouth. 'You mean *do*, don't you, Melanie? I seem to recall that your protests meant very little in the past.'

'Bastard!' she cried, tears springing into her eyes.

He stared at her for a long moment, then groaned and cradled her head against him, stroking her hair and speaking to her in softly soothing words. 'Let's not punish each other like this. It's cruel. And it's futile.' His sigh was ragged. 'You have every right to your privacy, if that's what you want. And every right to live your life as you see fit. I won't keep on making things difficult for you, sweetheart. I promise. We'll just enjoy tonight for what it is, right?'

'Right,' she whispered back weakly, then shivered.

He pulled back, a wickedly sardonic smile curving his mouth to one side. 'Then let's drink up,' he said, and reached for the champagne. 'We have a lot of memories to pack into one short night!'

CHAPTER THIRTEEN

THE Ballroom at the Regency was a magnificent re-creation of some of the European ballrooms of the past, with mirror-panelled walls, elaborate gilt-edged frescos on the high domed ceilings and chandeliers so ornate and large that they must have been hoisted into place with cranes.

Melanie peered over the shoulders of the group of people standing in front of them, trying to distract her churning stomach by admiring the surroundings. She'd no idea each couple was going to be formally presented as they arrived and she felt sick with nerves.

'Stop looking so worried,' Royce whispered. 'There's not a woman here to touch you. You'll be the belle of the ball.'

Melanie blinked over at him. Did he honestly think it was her appearance she was worrying over? It was being here at *all* that was bothering her. She should have confessed to Ava and Byron she was coming.

Suddenly, there was nothing between herself and the roll of red carpet running right up the middle of the ballroom, along which each couple walked after being presented. Her eyes darted around the huge room, past the magnificently decorated banquet tables that lined the walls, down to where groups of people were gathered near the stage and the orchestra.

The first person Melanie saw was Byron, his wavy blue-black hair gleaming high above the two females flanking him. Jade was on his left, looking sensational as usual in a long scarlet strapless sheath. Ava stood on his right, very elegant in her cleverly draped cornflower-blue gown. Even her hair looked good, now that she'd had the frizzed ends cut off and the rest permed into a soft cap of golden-brown curls.

153

As Melanie watched them chatting away to each other, Kyle joined the threesome, bringing with him a couple of glasses of champagne. Gemma and Nathan were nowhere in sight.

The man whose job it was to present everyone stepped forward, dressed like a footman from the Regency period, with a powdered wig, red coat, white breeches and highly polished black boots. Royce handed him the gilt-edged tickets, whereupon the 'footman', after giving Melanie a highly appreciative look, assumed a suitably formal expression and announced in a loud, very Shakespearian voice, 'Presenting Mr Royce Grantham ... and Mrs Melanie Lloyd!'

Heads twisted, mostly to stare first at Royce—he was the celebrity, after all—then at his companion. One selected group, however, stared straight at Melanie.

'Good God,' Byron gasped. 'That can't be *our* Melanie Lloyd.'

Ava was totally speechless, an affliction that Jade rarely suffered from.

'It most assuredly is,' she confirmed, smiling ruefully at the sight of their normally drab housekeeper making her way slowly down the red carpet, looking like a film star on her way to collecting an Oscar. A very *sexy* film star...

'Mmm,' was Kyle's only comment, but it brought a jealous glare from his fiancée.

'Down, boy,' she hissed, and he chuckled.

'I don't believe it,' Byron was muttering. 'What is she doing here with Royce? I thought she'd turned him down that night after dinner.'

Ava finally found her voice. 'Oh, no, she went out with him. She told me. And he sent her flowers yesterday. Masses and masses of long-stemmed red roses. I was there when they arrived.'

Byron turned on his sister. 'You *know* about this ... liaison, and you didn't tell me?' he asked, sounding both amazed and annoyed.

'It ... it's not a l ... liaison, Byron,' Ava stammered. 'Melanie says it's a ... a friendship of convenience.'

'Good God, woman, open your silly eyes! No woman dresses like that for a simple bloody friendship!'

'Why so upset, Pops?' Jade queried archly. 'You wouldn't be jealous, would you?'

'Jealous? Why would I be jealous? Don't be ridiculous, Jade. I just don't like to see a nice woman like Melanie being taken advantage of by a man like Royce.'

'That's a fairly harsh judgement, Byron,' Kyle intervened smoothly. 'Your housekeeper is what? Thirty?'

'Thirty-two.'

'And a widow of some years?'

'Yes.'

'Then I doubt any man could take advantage of her, especially a man of Royce Grantham's obvious reputation. Mrs Lloyd strikes me as a lady who knows her own mind and wouldn't easily be fooled. I think she deserves more credit for common sense than you're giving her. If she's having an affair with Royce Grantham then it's because she wants to. She's a grown woman, Byron. And a very beautiful one. Did you think she was going to spend the rest of her life in total celibacy?'

'You don't know the whole story where Melanie is concerned,' Byron grumbled.

Now Jade was frowning. 'That's true, Kyle. She...oh, dear, they're coming over. Be nice, Pops. There's nothing to be gained by making things awkward, is there?'

'I guess not,' he muttered, and somehow found a charming smile for the new arrivals. After all, he couldn't really afford to alienate the main bidder for that infernal opal, could he? But it was to be hoped Royce would take both it and himself back to England tomorrow and leave Melanie alone. She deserved better, the poor woman.

Poor woman? Good God, she looked anything but poor tonight. She looked glamorous and gorgeous, and so bloody sensual he couldn't take his eyes off her. A definite prickling in his loins brought him up with a jolt. Damn, but he would have to find himself a woman. And soon!

'Melanie,' he said warmly, extending his hands to take both of hers. 'What a dark horse you are, sneaking out to this ball like Cinderella! But what a glorious gown. And how stunning you look in it, my dear.' Dropping her hands, he turned to shake Royce's hand and deliver some more polite patter, even if he was still somewhat rattled inside.

Melanie smiled a stiff smile and looked nervously round the group. Ava was staring openly. Jade was frowning slightly. And Kyle was smiling, thank God.

'You do look stunning, Mrs Lloyd,' he said.

'Do call me Melanie.'

'Very well. You must save a dance for me later, Melanie. That is . . . if my gaoler here will give me the key for a while.'

Jade bestowed a very possessive look his way, linking her arm with his and clasping it tightly against her side. 'I never thought I'd have to protect my man from *your* clutches, Melanie.'

Melanie laughed. It was all rather funny, in a way. Byron had done his best to cover his shock but it had been there in his eyes. There'd been something else in his eyes as well which bothered her a little. The last thing she wanted was for *Byron* to start lusting after her.

'You look very beautiful, Melanie,' Ava said enviously.

'And so do you, Ava. Doesn't Ava look lovely tonight, everyone?'

Everyone said she did.

A sudden awkward silence descended on the group, and into that silence came an astonishing announcement.

'Presenting Mr Damian Campbell and Ms Celeste Campbell!'

A sound like rushing water rippled round the room as most people either gasped or murmured something. The ones who weren't staring with their mouths open, that was.

Melanie was as shocked as everyone else, her eyes flying to Byron to see what his reaction would be. But where she had expected him to be blustering with fury and outrage, he was actually ashen-faced. And ominously silent. He stood there, staring at the woman, as

were most people in the room by now, even the ones
who had no idea who she was.

There was no doubt Celeste Campbell was worth
staring at.

Rising forty, she looked at least ten years younger, her
striking face unwrinkled, her sultry mouth painted and
pouting, her long tawny blonde hair tumbling in glorious disarray around her shoulders and halfway down
her back. But it was her body that riveted all the men's
eyes, her tall athletic body, honed to perfection and out-
rageously displayed tonight in a dress that was both
spectacular and shocking at the same time.

Champagne in colour, it might have been sewn on, so
tightly was it fitted, following the curves of its female
wearer right down to her trim ankles and dainty feet,
which were sexily shod in gold sandals. The style was
basically strapless, with a sheer layer of champagne
chiffon that reached high round her neck and down her
arms to her wrists. This alone would have been quite
modest—despite the tightness—if it hadn't been for the
selected gold beading on the body of the gown.

From a distance the beading stood out, the rest of the
skin-coloured material taking on the appearance of bare
flesh. It looked as if she was wearing a very skimpy
costume, something like an exotic dancer would wear.
A small area of beads covered each nipple area, one large
bead rested over her navel, while more intense beading
formed a provocative V at the juncture of her thighs.

When she turned side-on—the sides did not have
beads—one gained a fleeting impression of nakedness
right up to her armpits. The back of the dress—easily
seen in the mirror panels on the wall as she walked up
the carpet—was sheer chiffon to where the beading began
on her buttocks. A slit right up to her bottom might
have been there for movement. But Melanie doubted it.
The legs on display were as sensational as the rest of her
body.

Melanie found it impossible to take her eyes off the
dress, and the woman in it. Royce, she fancied, was

similarly hypnotised since he hadn't moved an inch since sighting her.

'One has to admire her gall,' Jade said at last.

'I was admiring more than her gall,' Kyle added drily. 'That is *some* dress.'

'It's disgusting,' Byron snapped, reefing his eyes away at last. 'That woman's disgusting.'

'What's she doing here?' Ava whispered, still gaping.

'To spite me, no doubt,' Byron snarled. 'What else?'

'Who's that she's with?' Ava went on avidly. 'He's years younger than Celeste. I suppose he's her newest toy-boy lover.'

'For pity's sake, Ava,' Byron snapped. 'Weren't you listening just now? That's her snake of a brother, Damian. Don't stare at him!'

Melanie had not noticed the brother. She'd been too busy staring at Celeste Campbell. Her eyes went back to where Ms Campbell and her male companion had stopped to speak to a couple they obviously knew, and her breath caught. Dear God, but that was the most beautiful man she had ever seen.

Beautiful. But yes... Byron was right. There *was* something about him, something... slimy.

Was it the way his jet-black hair was slicked straight back from his forehead? Or the way his deeply set dark eyes were moving almost slyly around the room while he dragged on a cigarette?

Impossible to narrow it down to one thing. It was an overall impression.

His heavy-lidded gaze landed on her and she stiffened. He didn't smile. He simply stared. A chill invaded Melanie and she wrenched her eyes away with a shudder of revulsion.

'Something wrong, Melanie?' Royce whispered.

'No... no, I'm fine.' But she wasn't at all sure that she was. Could evil be projected across a room like air-waves? Or was she becoming fanciful? Maybe Byron's contemptuous description of the man had coloured her thoughts.

'Let me get you a drink,' Royce suggested. 'I can see one of those red-coated waiters coming our way. What would you like?'

'Oh—er—champagne would be nice.'

'Champagne coming up. Anyone else for a drink? Ava, your glass is nearly empty.'

Conversation revolved around what everyone was going to drink next. They all agreed on another champagne for this round.

'Oh, look,' Ava exclaimed after her first sip. 'It's Nathan and Gemma at last. Oh, doesn't Gemma look enchantingly pretty in that sweet dress?'

Now Melanie had never felt Gemma looked enchantingly pretty in anything. Her body was too lush and earthy, her face too exotic with its almond-shaped brown eyes, high cheekbones and generous mouth to be labelled 'pretty'. Still, that air of youthful innocence she unconsciously carried was still there—despite her marriage to Nathan—and that dress might have been virginally sweet on another less voluptuous female, so she could understand how Ava could be misled into such a description. Ava's own ingenuousness where sex was concerned lent a naïveté to her opinions that would not have been echoed by any of the men looking at Gemma at that precise moment.

A sudden thought struck Melanie and, very, very carefully, she snuck a glance over at Damian Campbell. Oh, my God, she thought, her stomach contracting. Just look at the way he's staring at her. No, not staring, *eating* her up with his eyes. Suddenly, Melanie felt afraid for Gemma, which was crazy really. Nathan was an extremely possessive husband, and not one to allow men like Damian Campbell anywhere near his lovely young wife. Just look at how he'd reacted to Royce going into the shop and asking her a few simple questions.

Still...

Her gaze returned to Gemma as Nathan guided her down the red carpet. She doesn't look happy, Melanie thought. And neither does Nathan. He dredged up one of his smooth smiles as he approached, though it stiffened once he saw Royce, then faded entirely to a look of shock once he recognised Melanie.

'Don't say it, Nathan,' Jade warned laughingly. 'We all have and Melanie's sick of it, aren't you?'

'That depends on what he says,' she smiled. 'Hello, Nathan . . . Gemma. What a lovely dress.'

There followed quite a bit of discussion over Gemma's dress, till Ava suddenly grabbed her brother's arm. 'Good God, Byron,' she hissed. 'Celeste's coming over. Oh, my goodness. Oh, heavens . . .'

'Pull yourself together, woman,' he growled, though the blood had drained from his face again, Melanie noted. What *was* it between these two?

'Good evening, everyone,' Celeste drawled as the group parted like the Red Sea for her arrival. Up close, she was even more beautiful, with the most unusually captivating eyes. Almost oriental in shape, they were a sherry-yellow in the middle, rimmed with a dark brown, and lashed thickly with long curly brown lashes. They were quite magnetic in their exotic feline beauty. Melanie could not stop staring at them.

When she did finally look away it was to find the others still staring at the woman with some interesting expressions on their faces. Byron, now that he'd had a moment to gather himself, was clearly furious. Ava was goggle-eyed. Jade was wryly admiring, while Kyle and Royce were simply wry, as though they recognised the type and were content just to look.

Gemma was the only one whose attention was not on Celeste Campbell, which was because she was frowning up at Nathan who, quite frankly, seemed the most uncomfortable of everyone. He was glaring at the woman with an expression bordering on explosive. Every muscle in his stiffly held body shouted an inner tension that was killing him.

'Byron, darling,' Celeste began silkily, not giving the rest of the group a single glance, let alone a word of greeting. Her eyes were all for Byron, only for Byron. 'It's so long since I've seen you. *Too* long. Not that I haven't got a bone to pick with you. What naughty person at Whitmore's has been spreading nasty rumours about Campbell's duty-free stores? Not you personally, I hope, though a little birdy told me it was. Truly, Byron, I didn't think you would stoop to such low tactics. Not a man of *your* honour.'

Did he wince at this last, barely hidden barb? Melanie couldn't be sure. He certainly seemed to stiffen slightly. Whatever his reaction, to give Byron credit, once he'd gathered himself, he was superb. 'You know what they say, Celeste,' he drawled. 'If you can't beat them, join them.'

'How divinely original! Are you saying you sincerely believe that I *do* give bribes and kickbacks as a normal business practice?' she delivered in a sweetly poisonous voice. 'Because if you do, and you say it out loud and in company, I might just have to take you to court for slander.'

'Do that,' he agreed without batting an eyelash.

'But before you do, Ms Campbell,' Kyle joined in in his usual cool fashion, 'I suggest you have a little chat with your sales and marketing manager.'

'Damian?' She flicked an eye over her shoulder to where her brother was still talking to the couple on the corner. 'Now why should I do that?' she asked nonchalantly, though anyone could see that Kyle had struck a raw nerve.

'Just a suggestion,' Kyle drawled.

His drily triumphant tone wiped the smile from her face. 'And who are *you*?' she asked curtly.

'He's Whitmore's brilliant new marketing manager,' Jade jumped in. 'Not to mention my fiancé.'

Those cat's eyes narrowed upon this young upstart in the red evening gown, then widened. '*Jade*? God, surely you're not little *Jade*!'

Jade drew herself up tall. 'I certainly am. But I'm not so little any more, Aunt Celeste.'

'Goodness, no,' Celeste returned drily. 'You certainly aren't. And haven't you done well for yourself?' she added huskily, appreciative eyes travelling over Kyle.

'What in hell are you doing here, Celeste?' Nathan suddenly snapped, jerking everyone's eyes his way. Nathan was usually so cool and composed. This wasn't like him at all.

Celeste turned to face him, her expression withering in its contempt. 'Well, well, well, if it isn't Byron's bad-boy-makes-good protégé. Yet this doesn't appear to be the wife I last saw you with...' She flicked a knowing look over Gemma. 'Exchanged her for a younger model, have you? How very predictable of you. But to answer your oh, so polite question, Nathan, this ball *was* open to anyone who purchased tickets, which I did. But I don't mind you knowing my main reason for coming here. I've come to get something back that belongs to me.'

'There's nothing here that belongs to you, Celeste,' Nathan flung at her, a cold fury in his eyes.

'Oh, really?' Celeste scorned. 'Then take a look at that opal up there on the stage in that display cabinet. The one with the security guards flanking it. At least *half* of that belongs to me. Or, more accurately, to the Campbell family. David Whitmore robbed my father of his share nearly forty years ago. Frankly, I'm intrigued to find out how it comes still to be in the possession of the Whitmores when it was reportedly stolen over twenty years before.' She swung back to face Byron, her eyebrows arching. 'Byron? I think I deserve an explanation.'

'What you deserve, Celeste,' he said darkly, 'is not fit for ears of the ladies present. I'll have you know that my father offered that opal to your father in 1945 gratis. But your father refused to take it.'

'That's a lie,' she countered icily. 'My father said your father cheated him while he was away, fighting for his country. And I believe him. No one hates that long and that well for *nothing*!'

Their eyes clashed, and everyone watching them knew that Celeste was no longer talking about their fathers but themselves. Celeste hated Byron, and it wasn't for nothing. Neither was it because of that opal.

'The Whitmores owe the Campbells nothing,' Byron bit out. 'You want the Heart of Fire back, Celeste? Then you bid for it! I'll find it rather ironic to fund some of the changes we're making at Whitmore's with Campbell money.'

Her cool voice was not matched by the fire still burning in those yellow eyes. 'My, my, I can see that Irene's passing hasn't sweetened your temper at all. And there I was, thinking you'd be a different man now that you were free of my appalling half-sister. My apologies, Jade, for speaking about your mother in such a fashion but you, better than anyone, must have known what a monster she was. Pity her husband didn't as well,' she finished savagely, and, turning on her heels, she departed as swiftly and angrily as her dress would allow.

Gemma stared after the woman, stunned. She'd heard a lot about Celeste Campbell, but the reality had far exceeded her expectations. The woman was outrageous in every way. And yet ... one had to admire her style, her spirit and her overwhelming self-assurance. There wouldn't be too many men who'd tell her what to do, or what to wear, or how to act. No, sirree!

'I'll buy that damned opal myself,' Nathan muttered, 'rather than let her have it. God, what an appalling woman she is!'

Byron threw him a surprised look. 'And since when did Ms Campbell deserve *your* derision? I always thought you rather admired her.'

'Admire that slut? You'd have to be joking. She's perversely amusing from a distance but I don't want to spend time breathing the same air she does. That goes for that lecherous brother of hers too. If he looks at Gemma one more time, I'll thump the bastard.'

'Nathan, he *hasn't* been looking at me at all,' Gemma sighed wearily.

'I think,' Kyle interrupted diplomatically, 'that the ushers are trying to direct people to their seats so that the banquet can be served. Shall we, darling?' he asked his fiancée, and steered her away.

Melanie was relieved that she and Royce were not seated right next to the Whitmores' group. Much as the interchange between them and Celeste Campbell had

been fascinating in a way, she could do without that sort
of tension tonight.

She almost enjoyed the meal, possibly drinking too
much wine, but the alcohol dulled the pain lurking deep
in her heart, making her light-headed and slightly silly.
She laughed at all of Royce's jokes, accepted his flir-
tatious comments and outrageous compliments without
making a single sarcastic retort and generally played the
role of agreeable female companion to perfection.

'I like you when you're happy,' Royce whispered into
her ear while she was spooning a brandied strawberry
into her mouth.

'And I wike you aw the time,' she said, the strawberry
in her mouth making it impossible to say 'l'. It sounded
so funny, she started to giggle.

He leant over and kissed her, prising open her lips and
taking the half-eaten strawberry right out of her mouth
into his. Her head jerked back to stare at him as he proceeded to eat it, stunned, yet aroused by the startling
intimacy of it all.

'You're looking at me like that again, woman,' he said
in a low voice. 'Don't do it, or I'll have to take you up
to my room right here and now. In fact, that's a splendid
idea.' He scraped back his chair and stood up, his sexy
blue eyes hard upon her. 'Coming?'

She gaped up at him, then snapped her mouth shut
and stood up as well. 'Yes.'

The triumph in his eyes brought a shiver of sexual
excitement. He took her hand and began to drag her
with unceremonious haste along behind the tables and
chairs.

'What...what if they auction the opal while we're
gone?' she whispered shakily once they were outside the
ballroom doors.

'Don't worry about the opal,' he replied thickly. 'I
have that matter well covered. Let's go.'

Gemma sat silently by Nathan's side, playing with her
dessert, moving the cream aside and searching for the
smallest strawberry. Seeing herself in this dress tonight

had made her wonder if she should try to lose some weight. Lenore was so slim ...

Suppressing a sigh, Gemma looked up and locked eyes with a man seated a fair way down the table on the opposite side. He winked saucily at her before she realised whom he was sitting next to. The infamous Celeste Campbell.

So this was the man who was supposed to have been ogling her obscenely earlier in the night, this incredibly handsome man with sparkling dark eyes and an open boyish grin. Yet Nathan had made him sound like Satan himself, probably because of his sister, who was, indeed, dressed in as scandalous a fashion as she was reputed to live her life. And there *she'd* been, worrying over a small amount of cleavage. Imagine how Nathan would have reacted if she'd come out in Celeste Campbell's dress.

And imagine how he would react if he noticed her looking down at the dreaded Damian Campbell!

Gemma dropped her eyes back to the strawberries and shifted them around some more. Truly, she had no appetite tonight. In fact, she felt generally wretched. What *was* she going to do about her marriage?

Nothing, she supposed. This was real life and real life was difficult at best. Hadn't she learnt that when she was a little girl? Why did she think falling in love would make it easier?

'You're not eating your dessert,' Nathan commented.

'No.' She stopped pretending and put down her spoon. 'I'm not hungry.'

'Or talkative. You haven't said a word to me since you sat down.'

'That should suit you, then,' she snapped. 'You don't like talking to me.'

'Certainly not in your present mood,' he grated out and turned away to speak to Byron on his left about the man they'd contracted today for the play.

Gemma made no attempt to listen. She hated that play and wanted to know nothing about it. And she hated Nathan tonight.

Feeling mutinous, she glanced down the table again in the direction of Damian Campbell, startled to find he was already looking at her. She felt an odd little flutter in her stomach when his smiling eyes narrowed to an intense gaze. And while there was something slightly disturbing about the way he was looking at her, it was also oddly compelling and she found it difficult to pull her eyes away. In fact, she couldn't, and soon she didn't even want to—

'Gemma!' Nathan snapped from beside her, and she jumped.

'W...what?'

'Ava was talking to you.'

'Oh...sorry...I...I...was daydreaming,' she said, feeling flustered and oddly guilty. What had happened just then? She couldn't quite understand it.

'Yes, Ava?' she asked distractedly, focusing at last on Byron's sister.

'I was wondering if you'd come shopping with me some time. Now that Nathan's so busy with the play you must have some spare time.'

'Oh, yes,' she said wearily. 'I have plenty of spare time.'

Had she said that loudly? Or did it fall into a momentary hush at the table? Whatever, her words seemed to echo around her ears, and when she slid a surreptitious glance down the table Damian Campbell's dark eyes were still intent upon her. A slow smile pulled on his attractive mouth and, before she could stop herself, Gemma was smiling back.

CHAPTER FOURTEEN

'GOOD evening, Mrs Whitmore.'

Gemma whirled as she let go of the ladies'-room door to stare down the corridor to a dimly lit corner in the distance. The red glow of a cigarette butt gleamed momentarily, just before Damian Campbell stepped out of the shadow into the light.

'Oh!' she exclaimed. 'It's you!'

He dropped the cigarette and crushed it underfoot. 'Come down here. I must speak to you privately for a moment. It's important.'

Gemma glanced nervously around, half expecting Nathan to materialise at any moment. 'I...I can't,' she whispered weakly.

'Why not? Won't the boss approve?'

'The boss? You mean Byron?'

'No, I mean your husband.'

'Nathan's not my boss!' she protested.

'Isn't he?' he said softly. 'I've never seen a wife so under the thumb. Or so nervy. Or so lonely.'

'I...I'm not any of those things. How dare you say such things to me?'

'I would dare to say a lot of things to you.'

She stared at him. 'What...what do you want?'

His laughter was low. 'Now that's a question. If I said a dance, would you dance with me?'

'I *can't*!'

'How about a quiet talk about anything you'd like to talk about?'

'No, I...I...'

'You can't,' he mocked. 'Better come down here, Mrs Whitmore,' he went on drily, 'before someone sees you already talking to me. Come on. I won't bite...'

167

Almost against her will, she found herself walking towards him, his darkly compelling gaze luring her on.

When she stopped short he reached out and drew her into an alcove, pressing her against the door-frame of a recessed door.

'What...what are you doing?' she protested breathlessly.

'Making sure your husband doesn't see us together, since that's what you're so afraid of.' He let her go to lean on the other side. 'Does he mistreat you?'

'No!' she cried, shocked.

'Oh, yes, I think he does. Maybe not with physical violence but in many subtle ways. You see, I know a lot about Nathan Whitmore. He's a twisted introvert, your husband. Not fit material as the life partner of a young vibrant woman like yourself. He'll stifle you, smother you, destroy you.'

'You're wrong!'

'Am I? We'll see.'

'Why are you saying these things to me?' she sobbed. 'They're wicked. And cruel.'

'Sometimes you have to be cruel to be kind. Look, I'm sorry if I've hurt you by speaking out, Mrs Whitmore. But I couldn't see you leave tonight without knowing that somewhere in this big bad city you have a friend. If you ever need one.'

'But I...I don't! I mean—'

'You will,' he interrupted firmly. 'How old are you, Gemma?'

'How...how did you know my name?'

'I know a lot of things about you.'

'But how?'

'This place is full of Whitmore employees. You've no idea how they like to gossip about their employer, and their employer's family. So, Gemma, how old are you? That's the one thing no one seemed sure of.'

'T...twenty.'

'Tch tch. And Nathan's what? Thirty-five, or -six?'

'What has Nathan's age got to do with anything?'

'It has everything to do with everything. You don't think he married you for your intellectual company, do you?'

Gemma stared at him.

'To be brutally frank, my dear, Nathan Whitmore does not love you. And one day soon you'll realise that. When you do, you'll need a friend, someone who can appreciate the beautiful, bright young woman that you are. The whole woman, not just the body.'

Her eyes had opened wider and wider with his coldly delivered yet oddly passionate words, her heart beating faster and faster.

'Yes, open your eyes to the truth, Gemma,' he went on relentlessly. 'Nathan Whitmore only wants you for one thing, and soon he won't even want you for that. I know his type. Believe me.'

'I don't believe you!' she cried. 'You're wrong. I won't listen to any more you've got to say. I won't!'

And she ran, back along the corridor, back into the ballroom where the milling throng of dancers covered her flight and her fluster. She slowed her steps, trying to cool her face so that by the time she rejoined Nathan at the table she would be fully composed. But she wasn't entirely, and he noticed, his glance one of dark suspicion.

'You were a long time in the powder-room. And you look flushed.'

'I . . . I'm finding it terribly hot in here. Do you think we could go home?' She stayed standing, hovering, hoping.

'It's really not that hot in here, Gemma. In fact, it's a little on the cool side.'

'Well, *I'm* hot!' she argued, knowing she sounded like a petulant child, but unable to stop herself. She had to get out of here. Had to! 'I want to go home, Nathan. If you won't take me, I'll take a taxi.'

He stared up at her, eyes narrowing. 'The auction's about to start. Do you think you could wait till it's over?'

'No.'

'Don't be ridiculous, Gemma. It won't take long.'

'Nathan, I don't ask you to do much for me but I'm asking you this. Please take me home.'

'I can't go home before the auction, Gemma. I'm going to bid.'

Her eyes flung wide. 'But *why*? Don't tell me it's just to stop Celeste Campbell getting the Heart of Fire! Who cares if she buys it? Why should it matter?'

'Would you keep your voice down?' he demanded impatiently.

'No, I won't! I'll speak as loudly as I damned well like. This is a free country.'

His frustrated sigh made her feel guilty. She was behaving *very* badly now, but something—was it fear that what Damian Campbell had said to her was true?—was driving her on. Maybe she was testing Nathan's love, trying to make him prove that his feelings for her went far beyond the physical.

'I was going to buy it for *you*, Gemma.'

Another present, she groaned silently, but with growing distress. I'm not a *real* wife. I'm little better than a mistress, to be soothed with gifts and side-tracked with smooth lies. Damian was right. Nathan does only want me for sex, and he doesn't even want me for that any more. Oh, God...

'Sit down, Gemma.'

She stared down at her husband, stared deep into his eyes and saw nothing but a reflection of her own misery and uncertainty in those implacable grey pools. Suddenly, all the other warnings people had given her about Nathan rushed back with a vengeance.

Gemma's head was beginning to whirl. Out of the corner of her eye she saw Damian Campbell return to his seat and, once again, she felt the need to get away from both him *and* Nathan. She needed time to think. She needed to breathe some clean fresh air.

'No, Nathan,' she said shakily but with a surprising amount of resolve. 'I am not sitting down. I am going home. You stay and bid for the opal, by all means. But if you're successful, don't bother giving it to me. I don't want it! I haven't wanted it since I found out my father stole it.'

'For God's sake, stop being so melodramatic,' Nathan ground out in a low, but clearly furious voice. 'That opal is your birthright and I want you to have it. Now, will you please sit down and stop making a scene in public?'

'Have you listened to a word I said, Nathan? I doubt it. I don't want to sit down. I don't want that rotten opal. I want to go home. *Now*!'

'Go, then,' he bit out. 'Don't let me stop you. All little girls should be home in bed by now, anyway.'

'Yes, they should,' she hissed back. 'But they shouldn't be sharing their beds with men old enough to be their fathers!'

Gemma's last glimpse of Nathan's face haunted her as she swept from the ballroom. God, but she'd hurt him. She'd really hurt him.

Go back, her heart whispered as she hurried on, out through the foyer of the hotel and towards the bank of taxis waiting just outside the main doors. Go back. Apologise. Kiss and make up.

But she didn't go back. She swept on, out of the hotel and into a taxi.

'We're just in time!' Royce said as they slipped back into the ballroom. 'The auction's starting. Let's stay and watch from back here.'

'But won't they have difficulty seeing you bid?'

'I'm not going to bid. I have an agent up front bidding for me. I've given him a ceiling.'

'What if Celeste Campbell goes higher?'

'Then she can have it.'

'But I thought . . . I thought . . .'

His gaze held a steely resolve. 'I came back to Sydney to secure only one treasure, Melanie, and she's standing right next to me. I love you, and I want to marry you. I don't care about the past, either yours or mine. I won't take no for an answer so you might as well just say yes.'

Melanie froze. How ironic that his final sentence contained the very same words Joel had used when he proposed to her. And right after he'd just made delicious love to her. Oh, with hindsight, it couldn't compare with what she'd just shared with Royce, but she hadn't known that back then. At the time, she'd thought Joel was an incredible lover. She'd been blinded by the sex and the charisma of the man, by his boldness and never-say-die determination. So she'd just said yes and in the end her blind faith in his love had cost her baby son his life.

How could she just say yes again, on so brief an acquaintance, even if she did yearn to do so? Maybe if it had just been herself then perhaps, yes, she would take the risk. But there was another child's life at stake. She or he deserved better than potentially divorced parents...

'I...I thought you were a confirmed bachelor,' she said.

'I was. Till I met you.'

'Royce, I...'

'Hear me out before you say no.'

She closed her eyes against the weakness already invading her.

'I love you,' he rasped into her ear. 'I know you don't believe me but it's true. I never meant to fall in love, never meant to take the risk of going through the hell my father went through. But all that went by the board the moment I set eyes on you, Melanie Lloyd. You love me too. I *know* you do.'

She opened her eyes and turned their luminescence upon him. 'Hush up, Royce,' she said softly. 'The bidding's starting.'

'Stuff the bidding! Come back upstairs with me.'

'No,' she said firmly, knowing that was where she was the weakest, in his arms. 'I want to see this. We...we can talk afterwards.'

'Oh, all right,' he grumbled. 'Might as well watch my own money being spent.'

Melanie was grateful to the auction for its distracting qualities. Bidding was spirited till the figure reached the million-dollar mark, then things slowed right down. When it finally passed one and a half million, Royce sighed.

'Well, that's me out. I'm no fool. The thing's not worth that much.'

'I wonder who's left in?' Melanie said, trying to see.

Royce craned his neck. 'Byron's bidding. And my God, so is Nathan! What's the matter with those two, bidding against each other? That's insane! No, there's someone else bidding as well. Not that Campbell woman, though. She's sitting perfectly still. Nathan's just dropped out. Byron hasn't. The man's lost his head! Hell, some idiot's bid two million.'

The auctioneer looked at Byron for a counter-bid but no, he was shaking his head. Melanie felt relieved, a sentiment echoed by Royce.

'Thank God Byron came to his senses in time. Whoever just bid that two million will be getting themselves a damned expensive trinket!'

'Two million once,' the auctioneer intoned pompously. 'Two million twice... Sold, for two million, to the gentleman over there.'

A balding gentleman rose, then turned to smile at Celeste Campbell, who got slowly to her feet, her expression triumphant.

'Oh-oh,' Melanie groaned.

Celeste mounted the stage to quite a few murmurs, mostly because of what the slit in the back of her dress was showing. When she reached the microphone she just stood there for a few moments, waiting like a golden goddess while her subjects gradually fell silent. Which they did.

'You are looking at one very happy lady,' she said in her slightly husky and very sexy voice. 'You may not know this, but the Heart of Fire was once owned jointly by the Whitmores and the Campbells, but through... circumstances... it became the sole property of the Whitmores. You may also not know that many many years ago, it mysteriously disappeared—presumed stolen. I, for one, was astonished to learn of its equally mysterious reappearance. But Mr Byron Whitmore seems content to leave that a mystery. Unless, of course, we can persuade him to come up here and enlighten us...'

Heads turned to Byron. Even from that distance, Melanie could see his face was like granite, his folded arms and wide-legged stance showing a controlled anger. Murmurs changed to clapping, and soon Byron was being urged on to the stage. He went with obvious reluctance and annoyance.

Celeste's pointy chin lifted as he approached, but for one who had invited this confrontation she was suddenly looking far from comfortable. Of course, Melanie could not see the expression in Byron's eyes as he mounted the steps, since his back was to everyone else. Still, she knew how formidable and intimidating Byron could be when his blood was up. And she could well imagine he was close to losing his temper.

Yet when he turned to face the curious crowd, his handsome face was lit up by a charismatic smile, his quite beautiful blue eyes glittering with what most people would have taken for indulgence or dry amusement. But a more intuitive onlooker might have seen a hint of malevolent intent, of an underlying hardness that bespoke hatred and fury.

'My dear Celeste,' he said smoothly into the microphone as she took an almost nervous step sidewards, 'I have long wanted to put to rest the ancient and quite erroneous rumours that a feud exists between our two families. All there is, folks, is a healthy competition between two similar businesses. Contrary to popular opinion, I am delighted that a Campbell has purchased our marvellous opal.'

'Really, Byron?' Celeste scoffed with a small smile, seemingly having recovered her composure. 'Which is why you were the underbidder, I suppose? Because you sincerely wanted me to have the Heart of Fire?'

Some muted gasps rippled through the room.

Byron's smile sent a shiver down Melanie's spine. She'd never seen him look so dangerously wicked.

'My dear lady,' he drawled, 'perhaps I was merely bluffing you into paying more. As for your other query... I wish I could relate a wildly romantic tale for everyone to hear about the opal's reappearance, but I'm afraid I cannot oblige. The tale is a very simple one. An old miner died recently and the opal was found in his possession, recognised, then returned to its rightful owner. The only mystery is how an opal stolen from my home here in Sydney turned up over twenty years later in the hands of an old derelict at Lightning Ridge. What do *you* think, Celeste? Could you supply a solution to this mystery?'

Celeste's frozen face was broken by a brittle laugh. 'What do I think? I think that's your story, Byron, and you're obviously going to stick to it.'

More laughter erupted from the ballroom. Byron grinned knowingly and said, 'True.'

Celeste looked furious and was about to say something else when a man in a black dinner suit and a black balaclava pulled over his head suddenly strode on to the stage. Everyone gasped when he put a pistol to Celeste's head, snaked an arm around her waist and dragged her to one side, well out of reach.

'It's all right, folks,' the masked man said with coldly controlled menace. 'I won't shoot Ms Campbell here if you all stay nice and quiet and don't move.'

There was a stunned silence when another balaclavaed criminal suddenly appeared on the stage, waving a lethal-looking rifle at the security guards while he disarmed them, then proceeded to put the Heart of Fire into a canvas sack along with the opal pendant sitting on the side-table that was to be presented to the belle of the ball later in the evening.

Melanie was as stunned as everyone else.

Byron, she noted, had gone a pasty shade of grey.

When someone pushed her own startled body away from the wall and jabbed something in the small of her back, it took a few seconds before she realised she had just been taken captive as well.

Royce was contemplating slipping through the back doors on his right to raise the alarm when a low voice whispered in his ear. 'Don't even think about it, mate. There's a gun pointed straight at your girlfriend here and if you move she's dead.'

He looked over and saw Melanie's wide frightened eyes and wanted to kill the bastard standing behind her. But how could he without endangering her life? He'd never felt so powerless. Or more sure that he loved this woman. God, if anything happened to her, he wouldn't want to live any more!

'Keep calm, everyone,' the head of the trio called out from the stage in his coolly arrogant voice. 'We're leaving now, but we're taking along a couple of hostages to make sure none of you does anything stupid till we're well clear. Come on, sweetheart,' he said to Celeste. 'We're *definitely* taking you. And my friend has chosen another delectable little honey from down in the back, in case all you distant folks are thinking of doing something foolish.'

Heads swivelled to see a pale-faced Melanie being pushed towards the back doors by her captor. Royce groaned his frustration. What should he do? What *could* he do? If he made a move, Melanie might be killed. Yet he'd heard experts advise never to let a criminal take a person away from the scene of the original crime. Experience spelled out that the danger to their personal safety increased with that move. But dammit, the gun was rammed right in her back!

The other two gunmen were by now making their way down the steps of the stage, Celeste Campbell in front of them. An equally frustrated-looking Byron stared after them, clearly appalled at what was happening.

When Celeste hesitated at the foot of the steps her kidnapper pushed her roughly ahead of them so that she stumbled to her knees. Gasps of horror punctuated the hushed room when he viciously yanked her upright by the hair.

It was then that the most astonishing thing happened. Celeste Campbell spun round with a cry of raw rage, her body lifting from the ground, her left leg sweeping round in an arc so quick and so expert that all the onlookers could do was gasp. Her assailant was rendered unconscious with one karate kick to the head, and within seconds the second man fell to a similar blow.

Unfortunately, the third man, the man with the gun at Melanie's back, was some distance from everyone and had pulled Melanie round in front of him for protection. Royce saw the man's panicky agitation at what was happening, heard him cock the gun. There was a loud crack, and a red flower bloomed in Melanie's upper chest. Her arms flung wide as she lurched forward, as did her eyes and her mouth. She twisted to stare blankly at Royce as she crashed to the ground, and he cried out his anguish. In a wild fury, he wrenched the gun away from her assailant and smashed his fist into the masked face. Smashed it again and again till he crumpled.

But it was all too late. Too late.

'Melanie,' he moaned, sinking to the floor and scooping her limp body up in his arms. Tears flooded his eyes at her deathly stillness. 'Oh, my love...my love...'

Royce sat alone in the waiting-room, anguished and ill. It was four in the morning and he'd been back from the police station for over an hour, waiting for word of Melanie.

'She's in Theatre,' the night sister told him when he arrived. 'The surgeon will speak to you as soon as he's finished, Mr Lloyd.'

Royce had not bothered to correct the nurse's misconception of his identity. What did it matter who she thought he was?

Jumping up, he began to pace. Maybe he should ring Frieda and Melanie's brother. No, better to wait. Why wake them up and worry them when they couldn't even see her? Maybe, in a short while, he'd have good news. Then, he'd ring them.

He swung round at the sound of the door opening. But it wasn't a doctor entering. It was Byron, looking every one of his forty-nine years.

'God,' Byron sighed. 'What a night. The police have finally let Celeste go home. Not that she hasn't stood up to the ordeal quite well. That's one tough woman, I can tell you. And an amazing one. Who would have believed she was a martial arts expert?'

'Pity she chose that moment to demonstrate her skill,' Royce bit out. 'Because of her, Melanie could be dying.'

'That's a bit harsh, Royce. Celeste simply reacted to the treatment that bastard was handing out. She didn't stop to think. And Melanie's not going to die. The sister at the desk has just told me the operation went well. The doctor will be in to see you shortly.'

Royce's shoulders sagged with relief. 'Thank God.'

'You look as if you could do with a cup of coffee,' Byron said, and made his way over to the automatic drinks machine.

'No, thanks. I couldn't drink a thing.'

'No? Well, I think I'll have one.'

It was while Byron was getting himself a hot drink that a harried-looking, green-robed individual strode in. He looked appallingly young to be a surgeon, Royce thought. Or was it that he felt appallingly old?

'Mr Lloyd?' he asked, glancing from one man to the other.

Royce stepped forward, still not in the mood to explain anything. Better they keep thinking he was Melanie's husband. That way, he'd find out everything he wanted to know. 'That's me,' he said, hoping his firm tone would keep Byron's mouth shut.

'Your wife's doing quite well, Mr Lloyd,' the doctor told Royce. 'The bullet punctured her left lung and ripped through quite a bit of bone and tissue, but fortunately it missed her heart and the major blood vessels. She's resting quite comfortably and you should be able to see her shortly.'

'Then she's completely out of danger?' he asked, still shaken by the storm of emotion inside him. 'I mean . . . Everything's going to be all right? Absolutely everything?'

'If it's the baby you're worried about, Mr Lloyd, then let me put your mind at rest. Everything's fine in that department too.'

Royce swayed on his feet, grasping at the doctor's arms. 'Baby? Melanie's having a *baby*?'

'Good God, man, you didn't know? She's talked of nothing else, even under the anaesthetic. We had to save her baby. That was all that mattered.'

'Oh, God...' Royce spun away, his head dropping into his hands.

The doctor placed a hand on his shoulder. 'I'm sorry. I didn't realise she hadn't told you yet. Perhaps you'd better not let on that you know till she tells you. We certainly don't want her upset just now, do we?'

Royce's nod was grim, his heart in turmoil. A baby... Dear God... And she wasn't going to tell him...

'I'll send a nurse in when you can see her,' the doctor said, and made a discreet departure, leaving Royce with his churning thoughts. He didn't understand how it could have happened. Or when?

And then he realised. On that Sunday...in the kitchen. She'd been very upset afterwards... He'd thought she was on the Pill, when clearly she hadn't been. She'd used some other method the night before, a method which was no longer protecting her that morning.

'I ought to throw this coffee in your face, you bastard,' Byron ground out.

Royce's head jerked up and around, distressed eyes slowly hardening when he saw Byron's fury. 'Don't jump to conclusions, Byron. This is not what you think.'

'You mean it's *not* some worldly womanising bastard taking advantage of a lonely woman? And what would have happened if *this* hadn't happened tonight? You'd have been winging your way back to England tomorrow without a damned care in the world, while poor Melanie's life will have been destroyed once again!'

'That's not true! I told Melanie I loved her tonight and I asked her to marry me. I am *not* going to go back to England tomorrow. I cancelled my flight the moment she agreed to come to the ball with me, the moment she gave me the chance to prove to her how much I love and want her.'

'My God, you actually almost sound sincere!'

'I *am* sincere, dammit. And if there's anything you know about Melanie that you think I should know then tell me, man. *Help* me! She's having my baby, for pity's sake.'

Byron's frown was troubled, then pensive. 'Melanie's a very tragic lady,' he said slowly, 'with a very tragic past.'

'I've gathered that, but she won't tell me anything. She loves me, Byron, I'm sure of it, but she refuses to trust me.'

'That's understandable. I think she would have trouble trusting *any* man, let alone someone of your reputation. But that's beside the point. You can't change your past any more than Melanie can change hers. In the circumstances, however, I think you have a right to know what you're up against.'

He dragged in a deep breath then launched forth. 'When Melanie answered the advertisement I put in the paper for a housekeeper over two years ago, she actually told me very little about herself except that her husband and baby son had been killed in a car accident two years previously, and that she hadn't had a job since. Most of my knowledge of her past comes from a private telephone conversation I had with her brother, Ron. Have you met him?'

Royce shook his head in the negative. 'I have met his wife, Frieda, and his son, Wayne, but Ron's been out every time I've been to the house.'

'Pity. Ron might have filled you in on things. He's no gossip but he does care about his sister. He only told me the sordid details because I'd hired her for a live-in position.'

'Good God, I knew that bastard of a husband had done something bad to her,' Royce muttered.

'That bastard,' Byron continued, 'went by the name of Joel Lloyd. He was an ambitious and reasonably successful advertising executive, handsome as the devil and a good ten years older than Melanie. They met when she joined his company as a receptionist at the tender age of nineteen. Apparently he swept her off her feet, married her within months, made her stop work, then proceeded to turn her into the perfect executive wife.

She took lessons in everything, from grooming to interior decorating to cooking to floral arrangements. Ron hated him, said he was all show and no substance, though he admitted he had style and charm and more hide than a herd of elephants.

'The marriage seemed happy enough, however, till Melanie started wanting a baby. Joel kept putting her off. Years went by, so one day Melanie just went ahead and got pregnant, and, surprisingly, once presented with the baby her husband was tickled pink. Adored the child apparently. They called him Peter. But then things started going wrong in his career, and dear Joel became a cocaine addict. No one's sure which came first. It came out at the inquest that he'd also been having affairs since shortly after his honeymoon, though he'd hidden them well. Melanie had found out not long before his death about the coke but not the women. Worried about him one day, she came to the office and caught him in some store-room having sex with the mail girl.'

'Hell.'

'The story goes she didn't say a word, simply went home and started packing. Joel came barging home after her, screaming all sorts of verbal abuse and warning her not to take the child. When she picked the baby up and went to leave, he snatched the child out of her arms, shouting that if he couldn't have the child, then neither could she. He threw the baby into the front seat of his car, and drove off at breakneck speed. Melanie was running after him down the street when the car veered off the road and straight into a telegraph pole. It exploded into flames on impact and she had to watch while her husband and baby were incinerated right in front of her eyes. Apparently, she had a severe emotional breakdown afterwards.'

'My God, no wonder. And no wonder she lost faith in men. I...I wish I'd known some of this earlier...'

'Would it have changed anything, I wonder?' Byron said with a sigh. 'Knowing things about a woman doesn't seem to change how you feel about them, or how you act with them. Lust has a way of making bastards of the best of men.'

'What I feel for Melanie is not just lust,' Royce denied heatedly. 'I love the woman more than life itself.'

'Perhaps you do, Royce. Perhaps you do. And Melanie must love you to have your child. I would have sworn she would never have a child again. Who knows? Maybe she *is* ready to live again. With you.'

'God, I hope so.'

'But if you ever hurt her,' Byron warned darkly, 'you'll have me to answer to.'

An efficient-looking nurse bustled in. 'Mr Lloyd?' he directed straight at Royce, who nodded. 'Doctor says you can see your wife now. Come with me, please.'

'I'll go home, Royce. Ava will be worried sick. Ring me if there are any changes and don't forget to contact Melanie's family.'

'I won't.'

Royce's heart turned over when he saw her. She was so pale and still, a tube running from her arm to one of those plastic fluid bags. 'Is... is she awake?' he whispered.

Before the nurse could answer, Melanie's eyelids fluttered, then lifted, revealing those beautiful black eyes of hers. But how haunted they looked with those deep black rings under them.

'I'm awake,' she croaked.

'Just a few minutes,' the nurse warned, and left the room.

Royce pulled up a chair on the side without the tube and picked up her hand. How cold it felt, and how frail. 'You're going to be all right,' he said, trying to rub some warmth into the hand.

Her weak smile moved him. 'And you're going to miss your plane.'

'The next plane I catch for England,' he told her gently, 'will be with you by my side, as my wife.'

She closed her eyes for a few seconds then opened them again. They were wet.

A huge lump filled Royce's throat and he just couldn't speak.

'I . . . I think I have something to tell you,' she said at last. 'I . . . hope you won't be angry with me.'

Royce swallowed and forced himself to speak. 'I could never be angry with you, Melanie...darling...you don't have to say a word, I know about the baby. The doctor let it slip, and I'm so happy I could burst.'

'But you...you don't understand... You don't know...'

'I know about everything and I understand everything. All I can say is that I *do* love you, darling. Really truly love you. When I thought you might die I wanted to die myself. You're all I will ever want. You and our child, and perhaps some more children. Would you like that?'

She nodded, tears spilling over to run down her cheeks. Royce battled to keep his own eyes from flooding.

'Making my family happy is going to be my next goal,' he promised. 'And it will be the best ever goal in the world because it will never end. Say you'll marry me, darling. I'll die if you don't.'

Her smile widened a little. 'Well, we can't have that, can we?'

His heart turned over. Oh, my beautiful Melanie. My beautiful brave Melanie. How could anyone have hurt you like that? I'll make it up to you, my darling, all the days of my life. He lifted her hand to his lips and kissed it.

'I love you,' he said in a strangled tone.

Melanie closed her eyes, her heart swelling with an emotion she thought she would never feel again. Not just love, but faith. This man truly loved her. She knew it. She *felt* it. It was real.

It had taken a near tragedy to make her see the truth clearly. With the danger had come a certain clarity of mind. She'd known, in those few seconds before she lost consciousness back in that ballroom, when she'd thought she was going to die, that if she had a second chance, if God was good enough to give her that, she would grasp it with both hands.

Her eyes opened and she smiled up at Royce, a dazzling smile that came from the heart. 'And I love you, darling,' she said. '"Till death us do part".'

CHAPTER FIFTEEN

'WHAT'S the news?' Gemma asked anxiously when Nathan put down the phone. 'It sounded hopeful from here.'

'She's going to be all right.'

Gemma dropped down into the sofa, all the air rushing from her body. Suddenly, she started to cry.

'Gemma...darling...' Nathan sat down beside her and pulled her into his arms. Gemma went because she didn't have the strength to fight him any more. She'd wanted to fight him by the time he got home from the ball, the hours of anxious waiting obliterating any wish to make up. She'd paced the apartment, wondering where on earth he was and why he didn't come home. It was to be thanked Lenore hadn't been at the ball or she would have started imagining all sorts of things.

Then, shortly after three, the key had turned in the lock and she had stiffened, ready for the fray. But then she had seen his face and known that something dreadful had happened, something that made their squabbles seem insignificant.

The whole horrific tale had tumbled from his still shocked mouth and she'd listened to it all in appalled silence. They'd all been kept at the ball for ages by the police, after which he'd driven Ava home to Belleview for Byron because he had to go with Celeste down to the police station, being one of the main witnesses to the robbery and the aftermath. Nathan had returned to the police station where he'd waited till Byron was free to go, thinking Byron might need a lift home, but he wanted to go back to the hospital. By this time, Nathan had been thinking he'd better be getting home himself, Byron promising to ring as soon as he knew anything.

'I could do with a drink,' Nathan said with a ragged sigh after Gemma's weeping had subsided. 'I think you could do with one too.' He rose and went over to the well-appointed bar in the corner and poured them both a brandy, returning to give Gemma hers before slumping down in an armchair opposite with his. She sipped obediently, while wondering why he hadn't sat back down next to her.

'Byron says Melanie's expecting Royce Grantham's baby,' he said at last.

Gemma's teeth rattled against the glass before it dropped down to her lap. Her eyes were wide upon her husband's.

'He *says* he's going to marry her,' he added sceptically. 'He *says* he loves her.'

'Maybe he does,' she returned with more venom than she'd intended. 'Some men *do* fall in love, you know.'

Their eyes met and Gemma would have given the world to know what lay behind that cool grey gaze.

'I realise that. But rarely men like Royce Grantham. And never men like Damian Campbell,' he finished coldly.

'Why on earth not?' she defended, despite a guilty heat entering her cheeks. 'They're human beings too, aren't they? They're as capable of falling in love as . . . as you and me.'

'I suppose Royce could be,' he said, idly twirling the brandy balloon in his fingers. 'But not that bastard Campbell.'

'He speaks highly of you as well,' she snapped before she could bite her tongue.

Those silvery grey eyes darkened to slate. 'So the truth is out at last,' he drawled. 'He did speak to you, didn't he? When you were so long away at the Ladies' and you came back to the table, all hot and bothered. What did he say, Gemma? What clever line did he spin you?'

'Why should I answer your questions when you refuse to answer mine? Or when you *lie*?'

'When have I lied to you?'

'Earlier this evening when you said you wanted to make love to me. That was a lie.'

His steely gaze dropped to the rapid rise and fall of her breasts and her breath caught. Now he *was* looking at her with desire. She'd never be mistaken about *that* look. Worse, her body leapt in instant response. God, but he had her well trained, didn't he? Like a dog. One tug on the leash and she was panting to do his commands.

She watched with a dry mouth while he drained the glass and placed it down on a side-table, standing up and stretching out one of his hands. 'Come to bed,' he invited darkly. 'And I'll show you just how much I was lying.'

'No,' was her defiant reply, though inside she was quivering with an excited expectation.

'Don't play the coquette with me, Gemma,' he snapped, and, grabbing one of her hands, reefed her to her feet. Infuriated, she threw the rest of her brandy in his face, thrilling to his look of shock, then quavering to his answering fury.

'You little bitch,' he hissed. 'You'll be sorry you did that.' Knocking the glass out of her hand, he gripped the back of her head and kissed her savagely, forcing her lips open and thrusting his tongue inside her gasping mouth. Amazingly, and for the first time, Gemma experienced a hot stab of arousal at this display of male aggression.

Her moan was one of raw desire. But perhaps it sounded like something else, for suddenly, Nathan jerked his head upwards, his face twisting with self-disgust. And bitter remorse. His eyes fastened on her still parted, still panting lips, then lifted to where her eyes began searching his with a stunned bewilderment.

For she wanted him to ravish her just now. Ravish...not make love. Wanted him to be rough. To take, and not ask. To demand, and not draw back.

Her groan showed true torment, and she spun away, lest he see the truth in her eyes. Instinct warned her that Nathan would hate her to have wanted something like that. He would rather she be boring in bed than de-praved. And it was depraved, wasn't it, to want your husband virtually to rape you?

His hands curled over her shoulders and drew her back against him.

'I . . . I'm sorry,' he murmured thickly. 'Forgive me.'

She could feel his hot breath on her neck, and her body ached to whirl in his arms, to pull his mouth back down on hers, to propel him back into that mad whirlpool of passion. But she didn't. She stayed frozen in his arms, every muscle straining to keep herself in check. She flinched when his fingertips momentarily bit into her flesh, then shuddered when he released her.

'Go to bed,' he said in a hollow voice. 'It's been a long day and you must be tired.'

She went, thoroughly ashamed, not only about herself, but of all the doubts she'd been harbouring about Nathan's love. If he'd married her for lust alone, he wouldn't have stopped just now. Damian Campbell was wrong. Nathan loved her. Really loved her. God, what a fool she'd been tonight. What a silly little fool!

A long time later Nathan walked into the bedroom to stare down at his sleeping bride. His darkly brooding gaze gradually turned to one of black resolve, and he turned, walking with quiet footsteps over to Gemma's dressing-table. Taking the three packets of pills from the top drawer, he took them out to the kitchen and ground each one down the garbage disposal.

She wanted a baby? Well, he would give her one. He would give her anything she wanted to keep her in his bed. Anything!

Take 4 bestselling love stories FREE

Plus get a FREE surprise gift!

Become a Privileged Woman,
You'll be entitled to all these Free Benefits. And Free Gifts, too.

To thank you for buying our books, we've designed an exclusive FREE program called *PAGES & PRIVILEGES™*. You can enroll with just one Proof of Purchase, and get the kind of luxuries that, until now, you could only read about.

BIG HOTEL DISCOUNTS

A privileged woman stays in the finest hotels. And so can you—at up to 60% off! Imagine standing in a hotel check-in line and watching as the guest in front of you pays $150 for the same room that's only costing you $60. Your *Pages & Privileges* discounts are good at Sheraton, Marriott, Best Western, Hyatt and thousands of other fine hotels all over the U.S., Canada and Europe.

FREE DISCOUNT TRAVEL SERVICE

A privileged woman is always jetting to romantic places. When <u>you</u> fly, just make one phone call for the lowest published airfare at time of booking— <u>or double the difference back!</u>

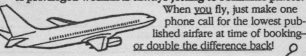

PLUS—you'll get a $25 voucher to use the first time you book a flight AND <u>5% cash back on every ticket you buy thereafter through the travel service!</u>

PROOF OF PURCHASE
Offer expires October 31, 1996

HP-PP5S